HIDDEN

Steven Lundle

Copyright © 2021 Steven Lundle

All rights reserved

The characters and events portrayed in this book are fictitious. Any similarity to real persons, living or dead, is coincidental and not intended by the author.

No part of this book may be reproduced, or stored in a retrieval system, or transmitted in any form or by any means, electronic, mechanical, photocopying, recording, or otherwise, without express written permission of the publisher.

ISBN-13: 9798461875732

Cover design by: Hedri

I dedicate this to everyone out there who has ever felt ashamed for being who they are. Remember that you are loved. Regardless of how others make you feel, your feelings and identity are valid. Things will get better.

CONTENTS

Title Page
Copyright
Dedication
Introduction
Chapter 1 — 1
Chapter 2 — 15
Chapter 3 — 27
Chapter 4 — 39
Chapter 5 — 52
Chapter 6 — 65
Chapter 7 — 77
Chapter 8 — 89
Acknowledgement — 101
About The Author — 103
Books In This Series — 105
Books By This Author — 107

INTRODUCTION

I wanted to start off by saying that I am overwhelmed by the support and positive feedback I received for my book, ASHAMED. Although it's a work of fiction, it's a very personal story, as my upbringing was very similar to that of Jeremiah's.

The first book dealt more with the feelings of guilt and confusion that Jeremiah felt about his sexuality; something I definitely experienced myself as well while growing up.

In this book, I dig up other aspects of my childhood. For example, how my family and school viewed the outside world at large, and even how there was a division among the various Christian groups. Some details may have been exaggerated or changed, but everything is inspired by some aspect of my childhood and upbringing.

This book is not an attack on my parents and their parenting style, but I want to showcase how this conservative style of upbringing often hurts kids, giving them a sense of worthlessness.

It has taken me years to get over how I was raised, but I am finally comfortable with who I am, and writing the ASHAMED series has been helpful in moving on.

Besides writing, I'm also an independent filmmaker. I am currently based in Phnom Penh, Cambodia I'm writing my first feature film, although work on that has been delayed by the Covid-19 pandemic.

Please check out my website.
https://stevenlundle.com

I blog there, and you can find links to all of my relevant social media. You can check out my short films too :)

Thansk again for all of your support and I will see you in my next book.

CHAPTER 1

I opened my eyes. Everything was quiet. I turned over to look at my bedside clock. It read 5:00 AM. I laid my head back down on my pillow. I still had an hour before it was time to get ready for school. I rolled over and closed my eyes.

If I thought long and hard enough, I could see Ricky sleeping, his back facing me. That was probably the best night of my life. I can't explain it, but I felt content and at peace for the first time in quite a while. I remembered every moment before I drifted back to sleep.

Ricky was sleeping with his back to me. I scooted myself closer and wrapped my arm around him. His breathing was steady, and I knew he was drifting off to sleep. I remained awake for a few more minutes. I was still trying to process this. *Was it real? Did he really say he loved me?*

In the dark, I found his hand, which opened to accept mine. He gave mine a slight squeeze, and soon his grip loosened. He was sound asleep. I closed my eyes and savored his scent and warmth.

The next morning, I was once again the first to wake up. My watch read 6:00 AM. I looked over at Ricky. We were both lying on our backs, and he was on my arm, which was numb. I gave him a small push, just enough to pull my arm out. I laid back down and waited for the feeling to return to my limb. I looked him over, and it occurred to me that Ricky was even cuter than I previously thought.

His short black hair was growing out. His skin was dark, but his cheeks had a rosy appearance to them. He was shirtless and wore a pair of orange underwear. I was still shy about my body. I slept in a T-shirt and a pair of cotton pajama bottoms.

In the dim light, I surveyed his sleeping body, and I ran my hand along his stomach, gently rubbing him. I stopped at his navel and let my hand rest there for a moment. I inhaled deeply as I tried to process what was happening. *Were we more than friends?*

I was still very confused about my sexuality. I liked Ricky. I mean, I liked him a lot. But I was still aware of what the church taught. Being gay was a sin and people like that would burn in hell for all of eternity. I'd heard that preached about more than once.

A shudder went down my spine, and I pulled my hand away. I was confused. I rolled back onto my back and glanced up at the ceiling, as if the answer about what I should do would stare down at me. There was nothing.

In only two short hours, we'd go to church together. I would go back home with my family, and not able to see him again for an entire week.

I sighed and just laid there. I had so many thoughts running through my head.

My eyes jumped open again. This time it was to the sound of my alarm. It now read 6:15 AM. I groaned as I rolled out of bed and made my way to the bathroom.

Standing in front of my mirror, I pulled off my T-shirt and stared at reflection. For the first time, I noticed just how bad my acne was getting. I held up my finger to my cheek and ran it over my skin. I could feel the acne. Like little bumps all across my face.

Next, I twisted my torso and tried to get a good look at my back. There were a couple of sunspots and that was it. I was always skinny, but I didn't like how scrawny I looked. If I flexed my arms, I could almost see the small clumps of muscle on my biceps. That was something I had to work on.

I never had a crush on anyone before, and now I was trying to figure out if I was attractive or not. I leaned closer to the mirror and took a harder look at myself. My eyes ran up and down my face. I needed to do something about that acne.

I sighed, dropped my pants and underwear, kicked them into the corner, and stepped into the shower. As I let the hot water run over my body, I ran my eyes over my arms again. They seemed so smooth under the water. I flexed them. I really didn't have much muscle on my biceps. Nothing to write home about, anyway. I wasn't sure if there was anything about me that Ricky found desirable.

The school day started out as usual. We recited the Pledge of Allegiance to both the American Flag and the Christian Flag. A Bible reading followed. I gritted my teeth and stumbled through the awkwardness of the Old English in the King James Version. We then sang a hymn, said a prayer, and got down to business.

We did our work independently in small cubicles, similar to what you'd see at a telemarketing office. We did a few pages in our individual activity packs, and then would raise our flag to get the attention of the class monitor, who would give us permission to score our work.

Everyone was in the same room. From grade one all the way up to grade twelve. Everyone sat in silence and concentrated on their own work. Our school didn't hire teachers either, so parents would volunteer to come to help as "class monitors."

I plugged on with my work until lunchtime. I took a seat at the end of the long table, where we all sat for lunch. I glanced at the chair where Ricky used to sit. Until recently, he studied here with me, but his parents didn't appreciate the way the school operated, so they pulled him, and he was now happily attending the public school.

We always had great lunchtime conversations together. Now his spot was taken by some other kid. I couldn't even be bothered to ask his name. I just sat there and ate my lunch in silence.

It was forty-five minutes later that something happened. I sat quietly in my seat. Another five minutes and I'd clear up my mess and return to my desk. My thoughts were derailed by the commotion that I heard coming from *the Learning Center*, where we did our schoolwork.

Like everyone else near me, I stood and tried to get a better look. Mr. Johnson, our school principal, stood there, his face red with anger. He rarely lost his cool.

Beside him stood Mrs. Sparks. She was this old lady and everyone's least favorite monitor. Her grandkids attended the school. She was retired and bored at home, so she volunteered every day, much to our chagrin. She was the fiercest of all the staff. She had her hand gripped around the arm of one little boy. Jason, I think his name was. He was only about eight years old and was in tears.

Mrs. Spark released her grip on him, and he fell to his knees. Mr. Johnson bent down to look him in the eyes. He said, "One more time, I want you to tell us what you were doing in there?"

Jason refused to look up, but just shook his head as his tears dripped all over the floor. "This is your last warning," Mr. Johnson said. The hair on the back of my neck stood. There was something in his voice. This air of authority. Everyone knew not to cross him.

He repeated his question. "What were you doing in that room? You know you're not allowed to be in there." Jason's crying got louder, but he didn't say anything.

"You were playing with this, weren't you?" Mr. Johnson demanded as he took something from Mrs. Spark. It was an action figure. I wasn't into comic books much and couldn't place the character, but I knew it was something our school didn't approve of. Anything considered worldly got banned.

"N-n-no," Jason sputtered. He said something else, but his words were all garbled, and I couldn't make out what he said.

Mr. Johnson stood back up and he seemed to be calming down. He gave Mrs. Sparks a nod; she walked to the other side of the room and opened up a small cupboard along the wall. Upon seeing it, Jason's eyes went wide. He shook his head repeatedly, and he muttered in protest, but to no avail. Mr. Johnson scooped him up with one arm, hauled him over to the cupboard, and shoved him inside.

The banging from inside continued for about five minutes until it finally subsided. I took a deep breath as I turned back to clean up my things. What we just witnessed happened two or three times a year, but it never got easier to see.

Our school was full of punishments. Only last month, shortly before Christmas, they had caught me cheating, and I received a paddle to the ass in front of the entire school body. That event would stick with me into adulthood.

Sometimes, when Mr. Johnson's temper was pushed to its limit, he forwent formal discipline, and he took matters into his own hands. Sometimes he hit someone. As long as he didn't leave any visible marks, that was usually acceptable. No one would say anything. Sometimes he just locked a kid up for a timeout and that was exactly what happened this time. Usually, he'd allow you to come out after you admitted to what you did and apologized.

That happened to me once. I was ten and made the mistake of bringing my Pokémon cards to school. My parents didn't even know that I owned them and I got into even more trouble when I got home. That violated their *no occult* policy.

I sat down a few minutes later and got back to work. It was hard to concentrate with Jason's murmuring coming from the nearby cupboard.

I stared at the math problems that were staring back at me for about ten minutes before realizing my right hand was scribbling away. I glanced down. I was doodling a picture. It was Ricky and me, holding hands. It reminded me of how much I missed him. He used to sit two desks over from me. I looked in that direction. His desk sat empty, and I felt an ache in my chest. I looked back down at my drawing.

Heavy footsteps interrupted my thoughts when they were only a few desks away. As fast as I could, I shoved my drawing under my activity pack just as Mrs. Sparks appeared behind me. I didn't look at her, but I could sense the scowl I imagined was on her face. Sometimes I wondered if it was permanently etched onto her face.

"Making a bit of noise here, are we?" she snarled.

"Wha—what? No, no noise. I'm just working on my math problems." I awkwardly opened up my math pack to a page I already finished. She breathed down my neck for a moment before she muttered something under her breath and walked off.

I sighed and closed my book. Looking from side to side to ensure no one was looking, I slipped my drawing into my backpack, and then laid my head on my desk. I really missed Ricky, and it seemed like it would be an eternity before I could see him again.

That evening, while my mom was cooking, I asked her if I could call Ricky. I knew she would get suspicious if I made it a daily thing, but I really wanted to hear his voice. If I could hear it just once, I could make it through the rest of the week.

"Okay," she said. "But make it quick. Dinner is almost ready."

I gave a nod and took the phone off the receiver. I dialed his number and waited about ten seconds before his mom answered.

"Hello Mrs. Vergara," I said, trying to keep my voice casual. "Can I talk to Ricky, please?"

"Oh, I'm sorry dear," she replied. "He's not home. He's started taking Judo classes and won't be home until late." My heart dropped into my stomach. "Would you like me to take a message?" she asked.

"No, that's okay," I said. "I'll see him on Sunday," and I hung up. *Sunday really can't come fast enough,* I thought.

The next day at school, the day dragged on even slower. It was uneventful. No one got punished, so that was something to be thankful for. Nothing else happened either. I worked in silence and looked up at the clock every five minutes.

If I concentrated carefully, I could see Ricky sitting at his desk. He'd notice me smiling at him and would give me this big grin. A grin that would brighten up the room by its very presence.

Of course, when I blinked, no one was there. I wondered if anyone would take his place., This was a small school, and enrollments were down. Probably for the best. This school was absolutely horrendous. I knew better, but I again broached the subject with my mom on the drive home.

"Can I change schools, please? I want to go to the public school, with Ricky," I said.

My mom's lips stiffened for a brief moment as she kept her eyes on the road. "Why are you bringing this up all of a sudden?" she asked.

"It's not all of a sudden," I said as I looked down at the floor. I felt a hot flush rising. "I just would like to go somewhere where there are more kids my age."

"We've already told you; your father and I want you to get a proper Christian Education," she said. "The public school is run by the government, and what they teach goes against our values and beliefs."

"Well, our school is so small," I said. "The public school has a big gymnasium, as well as a library and a baseball pitch."

"A baseball pitch. Are you saying that you want to play baseball now?" I didn't say anything. I knew how ridiculous that sounded.

"You don't even like sports," my mom continued.

"Well... I like to read," I said. "They have their own library."

"Yea, a library full of trashy books that go against God and Christianity," she said.

"Not all of them," I said. "I—"

"This conversion is over," she interrupted me. "We've talked about it before, but I'm done. I don't want to hear another word about it."

It took all my willpower to not slam the front door off its hinges when I went into the house. My dad tried to intercept me as I made my way to my room.

"Hey bud, how was school?"

I cut his last word off as I slammed my bedroom door. I threw my backpack into the corner and jumped onto my bed, burying my head under my pillow.

It just wasn't fair. I felt stifled at my school, and it seemed like there would be no way out.

I stayed in my room until it was time for dinner. I hadn't even changed out of my uniform yet, but after hearing my dad call me to eat, I dropped my clothes on the floor and changed into a pair of gray sweatpants and a white muscle shirt.

Dinner was the regular fare, but still good. Beef stew and corn on the cob. I ate in silence as my siblings were excitedly telling my parents about a fun activity that they participated in at school. I just kept my head down and continued eating. I wasn't in the mood to talk to anyone.

My dad finished first as he worked the night shift at a local factory and he was preparing to head to work. I glanced over at my mom, but her lips were pursed as she just listened and nodded to my younger siblings' chatter. I knew I must have hit a nerve earlier.

After we finished eating and my dad left, I helped my mom to wash the dishes. On my way back to my room, she stopped me.

"Jeremiah, wait. I want to talk to you for a minute."

I swallowed hard as I slowly turned to look at her. "About what you said in the car. I know you want to go to a bigger school and be able to do more activities, but you have to understand that your dad and I aren't doing this to punish you. We really love you and believe that this is what's best for you."

I just nodded. There wasn't anything that I could say to change her mind, so why even bother saying anything? She stepped closer to me, and I just remained still.

"I realize you need to get out and spend more time with your friends. Do more things than you do now."

I didn't say anything, but nodded as I listened to her.

"Pastor James is trying to organize a Friday night youth group, and I told him I'd like for you to join."

I looked up at her. "Will Ricky be there too?"

"I don't know," she replied. "They're still coming to church on Sundays. I don't see why he wouldn't."

"Okay, I see," I said.

"Their first meeting is this week," my mom said. "You want to go and try it out? I think they're planning a games night."

"Yea, okay," I said as I turned and went back to my room.

The rest of the week continued to drag on. Nothing eventful happened. It still bummed me that Ricky wasn't there and so I ate my lunch alone every day. Then I found a quiet corner where I took out my Japanese book and studied.

I had been studying Japanese for a while now. Ever since I got into anime. My dream was to move to Japan when I turned eighteen and so I got a few language books from the library and began my self-study.

My town had a sister town in Japan and a group of High School students were coming to tour our town. I was hoping to meet them and try out my language skills.

Friday finally came, and I went to the youth meeting. It started at 6:00 PM and I arrived on time. I made my way downstairs to the Fellowship Area. This was my *Learning Center,* where I studied during the week. Now all the desks were sitting along the walls and various board games were sitting out.

There were only a few kids there. A couple from my school, another girl that went to the public school, but attended our church on Sundays, and a couple of boys that I've never seen before. I had been told that this youth group was also meant as a community outreach, so they advertised it around town hoping that some kids from non-Christian families would join as well.

Ricky hadn't arrived yet and so I took a seat in the corner and sat by myself. One boy picked up a ping-pong paddle and called me to go play with him. I shook my head.

I didn't know any of these kids well and didn't have any intention of getting to know them. I only came so that I could spend time with Ricky.

A couple boys got on with a game of ping-pong while one girl sat by herself with a set of playing cards. The other boys were running around playing some sort of wild high-energy game.

Slowly, a few more kids came in and I got up when Pastor James brought in the snacks. It was 6:30 and as I helped myself to some potato chips, I noticed him. Ricky was coming down the stairs. This was the first time I'd seen him since I slept at his house a week before.

He looked really cute, dressed in black pants and a blue hoodie. He walked over to me. My eyes met his, and we both smiled.

"Hey," he said.

"Hey," I replied. I wasn't sure what else to say, and I diverted my eyes. I waited so long to talk with him. There were so many things I wanted to say to him; so many things I wanted to talk about, but I couldn't say much here in front of these other kids.

We each grabbed a plate and helped ourselves to some snacks. We sat down with the other kids and ate until Pastor James called us over to form a circle on the floor.

Pastor James was young for a pastor. I gauged him to be about thirty-five. He was tall and skinny and sported a small goatee under his chin.

He was cool and friendly and seemed to get along well with the church's youth. But he was still—like most of the adults here—quite conservative in his beliefs. Recently he had given a sermon on homosexuality, and it wasn't positive. I remember squirming in the church pew. It was awkward.

There were about fifteen kids here. Almost exactly half boys and the other half girls. We all sat cross-legged on the carpeted floor.

"Good evening everyone," Pastor James began as he gave us all a warm smile. "How are you all doing tonight?"

"Fine," we replied in unison.

"Great," he said. "Welcome all to our first weekly youth group. We hope you will all continue to join us here every Friday night."

He then took a guitar that was sitting nearby and strung a few upbeat tunes that we all sang along to. Songs that I had sung all my life, but I could tell that the new kids weren't as familiar with them, and they struggled to follow along.

After the singing, Pastor James pulled out his large well-worn Bible and flipped it open.

"Today I want to read from the book of Philippians," he said. "Chapter four, verse eight." He glanced at us for a moment before he began reading. *"Finally, brethren, whatsoever things are true, whatsoever things are honest, whatsoever things are just, whatsoever things are pure, whatsoever things are lovely, whatsoever things are of good report; if there be any virtue, and if there be any praise, think on these things."*

I cringed as I listened to these words. Both my school and church believed in only using the King James Version of the Bible. Even at home, they forced me to read it. I found it outdated and archaic, but I wasn't allowed to read anything else. My church community believed that any other translation was heresy. My mom actually gave me a book to read that made the claim that non-KJV Bibles were a New Age plot to turn people away from God.

Besides that, this verse made me uncomfortable. My parents quoted it to me all the time as they didn't approve of the anime or the fantasy books that I liked. Sometimes I snuck them home from the library, but my parents were getting stricter so I hadn't been able to read any good books recently. I watched the occasional anime when I babysat my siblings because my mom was working and my dad was sleeping.

After the reading, Pastor James looked around at us with a smile on his face. "Can anyone tell me what this verse means?"

One girl raised her hand, and he nodded to her. "It means that we should only fill our minds with things that are good or pure," she said. I rolled my eyes. That was exactly how my mom explained it, too.

"That's right," Pastor James nodded. "But it goes further than this. We should reflect on this verse for every decision that we make. We should always consider whether or not something pleases God."

Everyone sat in silence and so he continued. "What kind of movies do we watch? Does it bring glory to God? Or is it full of violence and sex? Maybe some other impure things that we really shouldn't be watching?" As he said this, he looked at me for a fleeting moment. I quickly looked down at the floor. My mom talked to him about her disapproval of my tastes in books and TV. I felt as if he was directing this at me.

"What about the music we listen to? Does it contain vulgar language or perhaps encourage us to participate in activities that we know are wrong? This is something that we need to always be mindful of when we consume media."

The discussion continued for about fifteen minutes. A few kids participated in this conversation, but I sat there in awkward silence. When the study finally ended, we were dismissed to go play some games. There were a few stations set up with cards games, a ping-pong table, a chessboard, and a few other things.

I just glanced at Ricky, and he gave me a meaningful smile and nod. We waited until everyone was preoccupied with their activities, and then we snuck upstairs.

We made our way to the bathroom upstairs; it wouldn't get used as everyone was downstairs.

I stared at him for a moment. This was the first time we were alone since last Sunday. I couldn't stand it anymore and I jumped on him. With my arms around his neck, I pulled him in and our mouths met, leading to a long, drawn-out kiss. I held the back of his head with my hands as I met his eyes with mine before going in for another kiss.

This lasted for about ten minutes. We snuck back downstairs before anyone noticed us missing and we found a quiet corner to sit in. We picked up a deck of playing cards and played a game of *Go Fish*.

"I missed you," I told him.

"I missed you too," he replied. I was in love with his gorgeous smile. "My mom said that you called," he said. "I'm sorry I wasn't home. I started taking Judo classes now, so I'm busy in the evenings."

"It's okay," I replied with a shrug.

"Did you need something?" he asked me.

"I just wanted to talk," I said. "That's all. Nothing important."

He just smiled at me, and we continued our game.

"My birthday is coming up. I'd like to do something," I said to him after a few minutes.

"Cool," he replied. "Want to do another sleepover?"

"I'd love to," I said. "Do you think your mom would let me come over again?"

"She probably would," he said. "She adores you. But shouldn't we have the sleepover at your house? It is your birthday after all."

I looked down, embarrassed. "Well, yea, but my parents won't really let us do anything fun. We have more freedom at your house."

"Okay," he said. "I'll ask my mom and see what she thinks."

"Alright, I hope it'll be okay."

"Shouldn't you ask your parents too?" he asked.

"Yea, I suppose so," I said. That hadn't really occurred to me. Maybe I should ask them first. They'll be more difficult to convince than Mrs. Vergara.

"I'll talk to them later," I replied. "It's still over a month away, anyway."

My birthday was on February 26th. It was disappointing as I hated winter and the cold it brought. Most of my friends and even my siblings got to have barbecues for their birthday, or maybe even go camping or hiking. I had the misfortune of not really being able to do anything that I wanted. Usually, I'd have a few friends over and my mom would make a nice birthday dinner. I suggested going to the movies with my friends, but there weren't many movies that my parents approved of. None I'd want to watch, anyway.

This year, my birthday could be much better if I could spend it with Ricky. Even better if I could go to his house.

When it was time to go, I walked with Ricky outside to wait for our parents. It was a quiet but cold evening. We could have waited inside, but we wanted some privacy between the two of us.

We walked over and took a seat on a bench that was beside the parking lot.

"So, what are we now?" I asked him.

"What do you mean?"

"I mean, are we still friends?" I asked. "Or... are we more now?"

"That's a good question," he said as he stared at the ground. "I've been thinking about it and I'm not really sure."

"Oh," I replied, and I waited for a moment before I continued. "You know, for a moment, I was really struggling with what I was. Was I gay? Or just confused?"

He looked up at me, and our eyes met. "Honestly, I don't much care for labels. All I know is that I really like you. I love you, in fact. You're the best friend that I've ever had, and I hope we can be more."

It took me a moment before I could say anything. "I'd really like that. I want you to not just be my friend, but my... boyfriend."

In the dim light, I could see his cheeks go red. "Really?" he asked.

"I mean, only if you want to."

"I'd love that," he said, and then he took a quick look around to make sure no one was watching before he leaned in and gave me a gentle kiss on my lips.

I was beaming during the ride home. At times, my home life felt stifling, but I could forget all of that now. I had someone I loved and cared about. This was the first time I could think of it in this way, but... I had a boyfriend. So now, nothing could get me down.

CHAPTER 2

The weather hadn't warmed up much as we got into February. I didn't like winter in the slightest. It was wet and cold, and I just couldn't stand it. My birthday was coming up, and like always, it limited me to doing indoor activities.

School still dragged on as normal. I felt lonely seeing Ricky only twice a week. Once at church on Sunday and again at the Friday night youth meeting.

It was the first Sunday in February, and Ricky and I went for a walk outside the church building as we waited for our parents.

On this day we went to the local convenience store to buy a drink. It was only a block away, and the sun was out, so it wasn't too cold.

Once we were out of view of the church, I felt Ricky's hand slip into mine. He held on for only a couple of seconds before letting me go again. Our town was small, and we knew too many people. We couldn't risk anyone catching us showing any signs of intimacy.

We bought a soft drink and a chocolate bar each before heading back to the church.

"So, my birthday's only in three weeks," I said. "Did you talk to your mom yet?"

"Not yet," Ricky replied.

"It's okay," I said. "I'll talk to my parents today. Let's see what they say."

"Okay," Ricky said. "No problem."

We continued walking down the sidewalk, sidestepping a patch of ice. "How's school going?" I asked. I was jealous that he could go to the public school. I wanted to go with him, but my parents put their foot down on that.

"It's going well," he replied. "I'm having a lot of fun there and it's easier to study, too."

"I see," I said. I tried not to look too glum. I was happy that he was happy, and I didn't want to get his spirits down. Apparently, I wasn't very convincing.

"Don't feel too bad," he said. "It's not all perfect. Especially because you're not there with me. I really wish you could be."

"Yea, me too," I replied. "It's okay, don't worry about it. I'm just glad that you got out of this prison I'm stuck in. I can't wait until I'm eighteen. I'll run away. Run as far away as possible."

I felt Ricky put his hand on my shoulder. "Don't stress about it too much. Have you thought about asking your parents to let you come do Judo with me? It's a lot of fun. I think you'd enjoy it."

"I'll think about it," I said. "Doesn't really sound like my thing, though. I think it's interesting to read up about the history of martial arts, but practicing it is something different."

"Oh, come on," he insisted. "It's fun, and we could see each other more often too."

"That's a good point," I said. "Let me think about it. I doubt my parents would let me, anyway. They'll say that it's too violent."

"You gotta stop being so negative," Ricky replied. "Just take a chance. You never know."

"Yea, fair enough," I said. "Whatever. I'll think about that later. Now I'm thinking about how to talk to my mom about my birthday. I really hope that she'll let me spend it at your house."

During the drive home, both of my parents were having a lively discussion about Pastor James' sermon. Apparently, a teacher at a public school in a neighboring town had been reprimanded for leading her class in prayer. This attack on religious freedom in our country enraged our entire church community.

"Oh, but if they led the class in a Muslim prayer, I'm sure it would have been fine," my mom was telling my dad.

"Exactly," my dad said. "This isn't about the Separation of Church and State like they say. It's all about their acceptance of one belief while their hatred for Christianity shows. The gay pride parade goes off without a hitch too."

"You see, Jeremiah," my mom said as she turned to face me. "This is why we won't send you to the public school. They have become absolute cesspools of degeneracy. I hope your friend Ricky has a strong moral character because Christian kids that go to those schools face a lot of pressure to conform."

I just put my head down and didn't reply. There wasn't any point in arguing, and my parents were getting pretty heated about this. I wanted to ask about my birthday, but I waited until we got home.

I broached the subject over lunch. My parents continued their conversation, but had calmed down a little.

"So, um, my birthday is coming up," I said.

"Yes," my mom said. "Was there something in particular that you'd like to do?"

"Well, if it's okay, I'd like to spend the night at Ricky's again."

"Why do you want to go there for your birthday?" my dad asked. "You don't want to spend it with your family?"

"No, it's not that," I interjected. "I just really want to go hang out with him again. We had lots of fun last time."

"Well, why don't you invite him here?" my mom suggested. "Invite a few of your friends here for your birthday, and Ricky can sleep here too if it's okay with his mom."

"Will that be okay?" I asked. I'd rather go to his house, but if they let him sleep at my place, that would be an acceptable alternative.

"Sure," my dad said. "Invite him to spend the night, and ask some of your school friends to come for the day as well. If the lake's still frozen, maybe we can go ice skating or something?"

I nodded. It was better than nothing, so I'd ask Ricky the first chance I got. "There's one other thing," I asked. They both looked back at me. "Ricky started taking Judo and he asked if I wanted to join him."

"Judo?" my mom said. "Isn't that kind of violent?"

"Well," I said. "It is a martial art, but it's not about violence. It is more of a sport, and it teaches self-control and discipline too."

"A sport?" my dad said. "You don't even like sports."

"I want to try this, though," I said. "They offer two free trials. I can go twice and if I don't like it, then I'll stop."

Both of my parents exchanged looks. "We'll think about it," my mom said. "Let me talk with Mrs. Vergara first."

"Okay," I said as I helped myself to another ham and cheese bun. I didn't get a hard no, so that counted for something.

I had to wait almost a whole week, until Friday, before I could talk with Ricky again. It was during the youth meeting, and like usual, we found a quiet corner to talk.

"I talked with my parents," I started.

"What did they have to say?" he asked.

"She suggested you come to sleep at our house instead."

"Oh?" was all he said.

"She also wants me to invite a few other boys from school too," I continued.

"Like who?" he asked.

"Not sure yet," I said. "Still thinking about it. I don't really have any friends at school."

"Well, whoever you invite, don't bring Darren," Ricky said. "I can't stand that kid."

"Haha, definitely not," I laughed. "I don't like him either."

"Well," Ricky pressed. "Who will you ask?"

"I suppose Chris isn't too bad," I said. "We don't talk much, but he seems nice."

"What about Chad?" Ricky asked. "I kind of like him."

"Okay, I can ask him," I said. "And maybe Ethan? He seems cool. Now that you're not here anymore, I might start talking to him."

"What? Are you going to cheat on me?" Ricky asked.

I couldn't tell if he was joking or being serious, but I gave him a playful punch as I said, "No, not like that. And keep your voice down, would you?"

We looked around, but no one was in the vicinity, so we were safe. I suddenly felt this urge to lean over and kiss him, but I resisted the temptation.

The two weeks leading up to my birthday crept up on me and

before I knew it, I was going home Friday evening after the youth meeting. My birthday fell on a Saturday this year. The invites were sent out. I had four friends, including Ricky, coming over. Ricky would spend the night while the rest would stay just for the day.

Although I wasn't much of an outdoors person, my dad convinced me to take the boys ice skating. Ricky was from the Philippines, and this was his first winter here. He never skated before, so my parents thought it would be a great experience for him. Despite not liking sports, I wasn't a bad skater as I was forced to take lessons when I was younger.

Everyone arrived the next morning around 10:00 AM. Three of the boys were kids I knew from school. There was Chris, who was skinny and athletic, with cute blue eyes and curly hair. I didn't talk with him much, but he seemed friendly and would usually say hi to me in passing.

Then there was Chad. He was also nice, but I found him to be weird. He was from a broken home, but one of the church families adopted him. I was told to not pay much attention if he got hyper as that was an effect of the Fetal Alcohol Syndrome that he had.

Then there was Ethan. He was actually Pastor James' nephew. He was short and wore a pair of thick glasses. Much like me, he wasn't big into sports, but preferred to study or read a book.

All the boys were about my age, give or take a year or two. And then there was Ricky, my boyfriend. I got a shiver down my spine just thinking of that. *My boyfriend.*

I would rather that no one else came so that it would just be me and Ricky, but my mom was concerned that I didn't have many friends, so she made a big deal that I invited some other boys.

While we waited for lunch to be ready, we all went to my bedroom. I was the oldest of six children and was the only one with my own bedroom. I even had an ensuite bathroom and shower. I worried I would lose it when baby number seven came in May.

We all sat in a circle on the floor. Chris was the first one to speak. "So, what did you want to do for fun?"

"Not sure yet," I said, realizing just how awkward I was. "What did you guys want to do?"

"Do you have a video game system?" Chad asked. It surprised me that he was allowed to have one. Most of the families from our church frowned at such things.

"No," I said. "My mom won't let me have one. She says it's a waste of time."

"Oh," Chad said as he looked down.

"I brought Bible Power Cards," Ethan suggested. "Want to play?"

Bible Power Cards was a trading card game. They were developed in reaction to the sensation of many trading card games based on various anime shows, which were considered occultic in our conservative community.

"Yea, okay," I said. "Is that alright with everyone?"

Everyone nodded in agreement, and Ethan went to get the cards out of his backpack.

While we were playing, Chris said, "So, why didn't you invite any girls over?"

"I don't know," I said. "Didn't think of it. Why? Were you hoping they'd come?"

"Kind of," he replied, and winked at me. I wasn't sure what to make of that, but I shrugged it off and we continued playing.

We were about halfway through the game when the subject of girls was brought up again. "What is your type?" Chris asked no one in particular.

"Sorry?" I said.

"He's talking about girls," Chad laughed. "What is your type? What kind of girls do you like?"

"Oh," I said, feeling a little embarrassed. "I knew that."

"So... what is your type?" Chris asked again.

"I want someone who is a devoted Christian and will support me in my walk with Christ," Ethan said.

Chris and Chad both laughed at him. "Your uncle's the pastor," Chad said. "You have to say that."

"Well, it's true," Ethan replied sheepishly.

"I want a girl that's smoking hot," Chris said. "I want her to have long blonde hair and huge boobs."

I could tell that Ethan was feeling uncomfortable at hearing this, but the boys continued.

"I'm with Chris," Chad said. "I want the hottest girl that I can get. Like a supermodel." He used his hands to imitate a set of female breasts.

The boys all burst out in laughter as I glanced awkwardly at Ricky.

"What about you two?" Chris asked. "What is your type?"

"Oh, I don't really have a type," I said as I put my head down and tried to resume the game.

"We're not letting you off that easily," Chad said. "Give an answer."

"Well," I said as I thought for a moment. "I guess I would like someone who is very nice and kind."

"Is that it?" Chris asked.

"I mean…" I tried to look anywhere but at them. "It would be good if she was good-looking too."

"What about you Ricky?" Chad asked. "What kind of girl do you like?"

Ricky was much better at keeping his cool than I was. At every turn, he impressed me. He opened his mouth and was just about to give his answer when my mom stuck her head in the door. "Boys, lunch is ready," she said in her chirpy sing-song voice that she only reserved for visitors.

We left our cards where they were and went to the dinner table. It was a tradition for my mom to ask us what meal we wanted for our birthday meal. I requested one of my favorites, lasagna, and boy, did it smell good.

We all took our plates and helped ourselves to a generous serving, which was followed by a dessert of rhubarb crisp and vanilla ice cream. Another request of mine.

Once everyone ate their fill, we prepared ourselves to go out to the frozen lake down the road from our house where all the locals skate.

It was Ricky's first time. He didn't even own a pair of skates, but he fit into an old pair of mine.

Once we reached the ice, I jumped onto it and did a few quick laps around the pond before returning to the side. I didn't like winter or the cold, but there was something freeing about being able to fly across the ice like this.

I could tell by the look in Ricky's eyes that he didn't share in my enthusiasm. I reached out my hand to him. "Here," I said. "Let me help you."

I took him by the hand and slowly pulled him onto the ice. "Just keep your feet steady," I told him. "Don't look down at the ice. Look at me."

He did, and our eyes met. I really wanted to kiss him at that moment. If I closed my eyes, I could picture the two of us being out here at nighttime. Alone. Just the two of us, under a starry sky. That idea painted such a romantic image in my head.

We'd race around the pond, hand in hand, and after getting tired, I'd bring him in for an embrace and a kiss. We'd then sit down in the snow and look up at the stars above us.

"Hey, watch it!" Ricky said, snapping me out of my trance. I stopped and steadied him before he fell.

"You okay?" I asked.

"Yea," he said as he caught his balance.

"It's okay," I said. "Want to go again?"

He didn't reply, but nodded. I took his hands and started pulling him again. He was unsteady on his feet at first, but slowly he moved on his own. I smiled at him, but he didn't return my glance. He was too busy concentrating on what he was doing.

He went at a steady pace and continued moving on his own. I loved that look in his eyes as he realized his own accomplishment. As he picked up speed and I continued skating backward. I slowly pulled my hands out of his. At first, I was within arm's reach. Then I backed up further, so that there were about two feet between the two of us. Three feet. Then four feet.

Just as I was about to step to the side and let him go on his own, he slipped. I reached for him and the two of us fell over onto the solid ice.

At first, I thought I broke something. Then I realized I had just twisted my arm under my back. I pulled it out, and the pain stopped. I looked up and Ricky's face was mere inches from my own. He was sporting a big grin. He peeked to the side and then gave me a peck on the lips. I gave a loud laugh as I struggled to my feet before I helped Ricky up, too.

Chris skated over. "What's up with you guys?" he asked. "Frolicking in the snow like a couple of gay lovebirds?"

"Yea," Chad said as he came over. Then they both started chanting: "Jeremiah and Ricky, sitting in a tree. K-I-S-S-I-N-G. First comes love, then comes-"

"Shut up!" I yelled at them. I noticed that Ricky's face was beet red as he diverted his eyes. The boys were still smirking at us as we dusted the snow off of our clothes.

Back at the house, I noticed a bruise that was forming under my right knee. "Sorry about that," Ricky said.

"It's fine," I said, shrugging it off.

Even though I was fifteen, we still exchanged gifts at birthday parties, and so we did that before the kids went back home.

Ethan brought me a new teen study Bible. From Chad, I received a pack of Hockey Trading Cards. I wasn't interested in sports, but I said *thank you* all the same. Then, from Chris, I got an envelope with a ten-dollar bill inside. That was nice of him.

Finally, it was Ricky's turn. He gave me a new Japanese grammar book. I was planning on buying it, but hadn't saved the money yet.

"Thanks a lot," I said as I grinned at him. Then I felt the awkward stare of everyone else. "Thank you, everyone," I said. "These were all great gifts. Thanks so much."

The three boys left soon afterward, and it was just Ricky and me left. He joined us for dinner, which was leftover lasagna, but that was one of my favorite dishes, so I didn't complain.

It was getting late, so we prepared for bed once we finished eating.

Ricky was going to share my room, and my mom had already prepared some extra bedding for whichever one of us opted for the floor.

Once we were alone in my room, Ricky jumped on me and our mouths met with more force than we intended, but we had been waiting for that moment all day, so it was to be expected. We probably made out for close to ten minutes before he got off of me and took a seat on the edge of the bed next to me. We both looked at each other and smiled.

"I was going to shower," I said to him. "Or did you want to go first?"

He just smiled at me, leaned in, and gave me another kiss.

"Just go in," I said to him. "I'll wait here for you."

"Okay," he said as he pulled off his shirt. I looked over his smooth, tanned body. To me, it was absolute perfection, and I reached over to run my hand down his back. He smiled at me as he stood up and pulled his pants down. I looked at his dark camouflage-colored underwear. I still couldn't get over how comfortable he was changing in front of others. That was something I was trying to get over. Maybe this was the night?

I was still staring at the shape of his butt in his underwear when he pulled them down. Here he was, standing naked in my bedroom with only the two of us. "Do you have a towel that I can use?" he asked me. I snapped out of my trance, and I had to ask him to repeat himself.

"Yea, right here," I said as I stepped into my bathroom and pulled out an extra towel that I handed to him.

"Thanks," he said as he walked towards the shower. "Do you want to come in with me?"

My whole body seized up at the sound of this. "It's okay," I said as I stumbled over my words. "It's fine. My shower isn't that big. I'll go in after you," I said. That was a lie. It was plenty big enough, but his request took me by surprise and I suddenly felt extremely shy and self-conscious.

"Okay, suit yourself," he said to me as we went into the shower. I waited for him to finish. When he stepped out of the bathroom, he was running the towel through his hair. It never occurred to me how long his hair got since he left our school.

"Your turn," he said as he made his way to his bag and rummaged around for a fresh pair of underwear. "Are you still shy in front of me?" he asked, almost like it was a dare. I felt this strange sensation run through me. I had to prove that I wasn't such a prude, like how I was raised.

I stood up and took off my shirt, followed by my pants. I glanced over to see his reaction, and he was just staring at me with a big smile on his face.

"What?" I asked.

"Is this your first time changing in front of someone?" he asked.

"Maybe," I said.

"It is," he laughed. "I can tell."

"Whatever," I muttered as I put my thumbs in my underwear's waistband. I hesitated for a moment. This was the moment of truth. *Could I do it?*

Ricky was standing there in his underwear and not saying a word. Just staring at me. I sucked in a deep breath, and with one fell swoop, I pulled them down.

"Not bad," Ricky said, as he nodded. "Not bad at all." I was so red in the face that I felt like I was about to explode into flames.

"Well, uh, I'm going to take a shower now," I muttered to him.

"Go ahead," he said. "I'll be waiting here."

I spent more time in the shower than usual. It had probably been twenty minutes by the time I stepped out and looked at myself in my mirror. I brought my hand up to my face. I forgot to ask my mom to buy some cream to clear up my acne. I didn't have a lot, but it still bothered me.

I looked my body over from top to bottom and my eyes stopped at what was between my legs. Almost no one had seen it since I was a little child, and I now felt self-conscious about it. My parents raised me to be ashamed of my private parts, but I was trying to get over that.

Should I have shaved down there before he showed up? Maybe, but I didn't expect that he'd see it. The thought never crossed my mind. I didn't even have access to a razor, so not like I could do something at the moment, anyway.

I let out a sigh and opened the door, going back into my room. Ricky was sitting on the edge of my bed, flipping through a magazine. He hadn't put clothes on yet, and he looked at me. "Took you a long time," he said.

"I wanted to be clean for you," I said to him with a smirk as I went to my dresser and pulled out a fresh pair of underwear, followed by blue cotton pajamas.

"You still sleep in pajamas?" Ricky asked. "Just sleep in your underwear. It's more comfortable."

I considered that for a moment. "I can't," I said. "My mom won't be happy."

"Is she going to come in here while we're sleeping?" he asked.

He had a point. She probably wouldn't. I took in a deep breath and put my pajamas back. I was really stepping out of my comfort zone.

"So, who's sleeping on the floor?" Ricky asked, as I pulled on my underwear.

"I was thinking we could both sleep in my bed. It's big enough." I walked over to the wall and turned off the light and then crawled into bed beside Ricky. We both turned to face the other.

I could vaguely make out his face in the dim moonlight streaming in through my bedroom window. "I'm happy that you could spend the night," I said.

"Me too," he replied, and he snuggled closer to me.

"I love you," I whispered. I could barely say that out loud. It felt so surreal.

"I love you too," he replied. His mouth came up to meet mine, and we engaged in an extended kiss.

"Goodnight," he said to me as we broke apart.

"Goodnight," I said, and he turned over, his back to me. I got in close to him and wrapped my arm around him. I felt like his protector. I wanted him to feel safe and secure with me.

His skin was warm to the touch and soon his breathing became even and regulated as he drifted off to sleep. I joined him mere minutes later.

CHAPTER 3

Over a month had passed since Ricky spent the night at my house. It was now April, and the weather was getting warmer. The snow was almost completely melted, and you could hear the chirping birds early in the morning as you woke. I hated winter, so it was a welcoming sign that summer was on its way.

I found it much easier to get up and get ready for school in the morning when it wasn't below freezing outside. After school, I'd even happily go for a walk near my house. I just wish that Ricky could come with me. There was so much I wanted to talk to him about. I could only see him twice a week, Sunday at church and at Friday's youth meetings. That wasn't as much time as we wanted. I hoped to sign up for Judo, so that I could have another activity to participate in with him, but my parents didn't let me.

It was Sunday, April 3rd, and Ricky and I took a walk after church while our parents were talking. The weather was beautiful, and the sky was filled with bright sunshine. We wore only our light spring jackets. This was going to become our Sunday tradition if the weather remained warm like this.

Ricky's school was about a five-minute walk from the church, and we headed in that direction.

"Where are we going?" I asked.

"Just come here," he smiled at me. "I want to show you something."

We walked around to the back of his school, behind a large dumpster. It blocked us from the view of the street.

"What did you want to show me?" I asked, with a little smile on my face. I knew he was up to something.

Ricky took a quick glance from side to side before grabbing me, and he locked his lips with mine. We went at it for about two minutes before we broke apart in order to catch our breaths.

"Oh, you're naughty," I said to him with a wink.

"Is that a bad thing?" he laughed.

"I guess not," I said. "You want to grab a drink?"

"Yea, sure," he said.

There was a convenience store just across the street. We walked over, bought a couple of sodas, then went back to the school and took a seat on a nearby swing.

"I'm having a sleepover at my house this Friday night," Ricky said. "Can you come? It's for my birthday."

"Let me ask my mom," I said. I almost forgot about that. His birthday was two months after mine. He was about a year younger than me and was going to turn fourteen. "I hope that she'll let me," I continued. "It'll be a lot of fun."

"It will be," Ricky said. "I met some cool friends at my school. They'll come too."

"Oh," I said. "Well, I'll make sure not to tell my mom that. She thinks the kids at the public school are evil."

Ricky let out a soft giggle. "What's so funny?" I asked.

"Nothing," he said. "I just can't get over how strict your parents are."

"Yea, tell me about it," I said as I rolled my eyes.

"Anyway, I hope you can come," Ricky said. "We're going to rent a movie too. It'll be great."

"Okay, let me ask," I said, and I brought my soda up to my lips. We sat there in silence for a few minutes.

"Ask your parents if you can stay two nights," Ricky says. "I want us to go to the city again."

"Really?" I asked. "I'd love that."

Ricky glanced at his watch. "We'd better get back," he said.

I nodded in agreement, and we made our way back to the church.

On the way home, I broached the subject with my parents.

"So, it's Ricky's birthday next week," I began. "He asked me to come to his party this weekend."

"Who's going to be there?" my mom asked.

"Just his family," I said. "Maybe a couple of other kids from church, but I'm not sure."

"What are you guys planning to do?" she asked. I dreaded asking her to let me do something. She always made it feel like an interrogation.

"Just stay at his house," I said. "Eat pizza and play games. It's a sleepover too. He asked if I could spend the night on Friday."

"Okay," my mom said. "Let me talk to his mom and we'll think about it."

"Okay," I said.

I'm not sure how honest Mrs. Vergara was when she talked to my mom over the phone, but my parents agreed to let me go. For one night. I was disappointed that I couldn't stay for a second, but it was still better than nothing, and so I didn't protest.

On Friday morning, I got up early in order to pack my overnight bag. The plan was that I would go to Ricky's house directly after school. Our parents allowed us to skip the youth event just this one time.

As usual, when I was looking forward to something, school seemed to drag on and on. The only memorable moment of that day was during our midday Bible Study.

Ms. Anderson, one of our supervisors, led the Bible Study twice a week. On this particular day, she brought out a newspaper article for discussion.

"Today I want to talk about sexual immorality," she said. "I was reading in this morning's newspaper, and I found something interesting. According to this, forty-three percent of all teens between fifteen and nineteen have had sexual intercourse at least once."

She looked over at us as the silence became palpable. Ms. Anderson then continued. "The pregnancy rate among teens in the same age category is about three percent. Did you all know that?"

Again, there was a silence as everyone mulled these words over.

"In the Bible, God commands us to remain sexually pure. In the Bible, we read the following: *Flee fornication. Every sin that a man doeth is without the body; but he that committeth fornication sinneth against his own body.*"

She looked at us for a moment before continuing. "Do you know what this means?"

One of the older girls raised her hand. "It means that we shouldn't fornicate."

"That's right," Ms. Anderson said. "God calls us to remain pure until our wedding day and that any sexual act that we commit before then is a sin against God."

I shifted in my seat. I always felt uncomfortable when these verses were read. It's like they could see right through me and read my mind. I didn't like that.

"What should we do to stay pure?" Ms. Anderson asked. "What if a boy asks you to go on a date?"

I rolled my eyes at the tone in her voice when she said that. Most of the families here, mine included, wouldn't let any of their kids date, regardless of their age. Instead, we practiced courting. When they met the right person, they'd go on group outings until they knew each other enough to get engaged. Dating in the traditional sense wasn't allowed.

We talked about this for a half-hour. By the time I sat back down at my desk, I had a heavy sense of guilt hovering above me. *But why?* Ricky and I hadn't even done anything sexual, except for changing together. *What was there to feel guilty about?*

Maybe it was just habit, but I put my hands together and said a silent prayer. *Dear God, please keep me pure. Don't let me fall and sin against you. Amen.*

As I opened my eyes, I wasn't even sure if I meant the prayer or not, but it worked. The feeling of guilt lifted, so I picked up my pencil and continued my work for the day.

Ricky and his mom picked me up after school. We stopped at the video rental store on the way to their place.

"What movie do you want to see?" Ricky asked me.

"I don't know," I said. "It's your party after all."

He just laughed and picked up a video. "How about this one?"

It showed a scantily clad woman in a bikini standing in front of her sports car. I just rolled my eyes. "Oh, come on, it makes you horny," he said in a joking manner.

"Horny?" I said, but I quickly changed the subject. I didn't want to admit that I didn't know that word. "How about this one?" It was an anime that we were both into. The cover showed a couple of shirtless boys.

"Maybe," he grinned. "You are horny, aren't you?"

I was getting the gist of what he meant. "What? For an anime character?" I scoffed and laughed it off.

"The only thing is that my friends who are coming aren't much into anime," Ricky said, and we continued browsing the shelves.

Eventually, we decided on a horror film. I looked at the cover and knew my parents would never in a million years let me watch something like this. That was part of the excitement. I felt like a rebel.

After arriving at his house, I showered and changed. By the time I finished, his friends arrived. Four boys, all from the public school. I didn't know any of them, but it was obvious at first glance that my parents wouldn't approve of these kids.

The first boy I met was Carlos. His family was from Mexico, and in a town where pretty much everyone was white, everyone knew who his family was. He was noticeably tall and wore a hoodie with the emblem of a Death Metal band. He was in the Judo Club with Ricky too.

Next was Austin. He had blonde hair, and I could hear a Southern twang in his accent. He wore blue jeans with a large belt buckle. I was told that his family recently moved here from Texas, and they now owned a ranch just outside of town.

Eddy was Ricky's friend from his school's computer club. He was of average height and had brown curly hair with a pair of thick wire glasses.

The last boy I was introduced to was Albert. He was what I

could best describe as a jock. He was the star of the school's football team and was very popular among the girls. I was impressed that Ricky was making friends with such cool people.

Everyone was spending the night, so Mrs. Vergara laid out bedding for everyone in the living room. We ordered pizza and watched the movie once the food arrived.

This was my first sleepover with a group of kids, and I couldn't believe my luck. This was also my first time with a bunch of non-christian kids. I knew my parents wouldn't approve, and I prayed they wouldn't find out. This was something that I hoped we could do more often.

I wasn't into horror films and this movie was something that I wasn't prepared for. There was lots of blood and gore and a man who wore a leather mask. He went around carrying a large ax and murdered people at a campsite. My stomach twisted into knots every time the ax-murderer killed someone.

As we neared the end of the film, my hand found Ricky's in the dark. I looked up at him. From the flickering of light from the TV, I saw him laughing at the gruesome scenes. This was a new side of him. I wasn't sure if I liked it, but his hand accepted mine and I felt comfort in that.

When the movie ended, I could breathe easier. That wasn't something I wanted to watch again.

It was late. Almost 11:00 PM, and I was ready for bed, but the boys had something else in mind. Mrs. Vergara was asleep already, and it was Carlos who announced he had an idea for a late-night activity.

We all followed him into Ricky's room, and they locked the door behind us. Carlos then brought out a bottle from his bag.

I wasn't sure what was going on, but all the other kids seemed eager about something.

"Did you bring glasses?" Austin asked.

"Naw, it's alright," Carlos said. "We can just share the bottle. No one has any germs, do they?"

"What is it?" I asked as I looked at the dark bottle that Carlos presented. He just laughed.

"Would you like to be the first to have a go?" he asked me. I shook my head.

"I will," Albert said. "You guys are just being a bunch of pussies. This stuff's nothing." With that, he took a long gulp. He looked at us, laughed at the looks on our faces, and took a second drink.

"Damn, man, that stuff's expensive," Carlos said. "Save some for the rest of us." And he took the bottle back.

"I'll go next," Austin said, and he took the bottle. He sniffed it, hesitated for a moment, and then took a gulp. It was about half as much as what Albert had. He made a scrunched-up face, and then passed it to Carlos.

"What's with the face?" Carlos asked. "You're just a wuss." He didn't hesitate, but took a nice, big gulp of the clear liquid before handing it to Eddy. He looked as unsure as I felt.

"Come on, go ahead," Carlos said. "Don't be such a wuss. It's nothing."

He nodded and took a small sip. "Take more than that," Carlos said, and Eddy took another sip.

"Okay, that's good enough," Carlos said. "Ricky, it's your turn."

Ricky took it, smiled at me, and took a decent-sized amount. It sat in his mouth for a moment before he made a face as it went down his throat. Then it was my turn.

I took the bottle in my hand and looked it over. "Come on, hurry up," Carlos said. "I want another go at it."

I nodded and slowly brought the opening to my lips. I took a deep breath and tilted my head back. I don't remember how much I took at that moment, but I remember the feeling vividly. My throat seized up as the liquid burned. I suppressed the feeling, and I swallowed it, but it burned my esophagus as it made its way to my stomach. The face I made must have been a telltale sign of how I felt, because everyone burst into laughter.

"Shhh," Ricky warned them. "You'll wake my parents."

"Whatever," Carlos said. "Let me have that bottle," and he took another drink. I had a funny feeling emanating from my stomach.

"I have to go to the bathroom," I muttered as I dashed down the hallway. I made it just in time. As soon as the toilet seat was open, my stomach erupted like a volcano and I emptied what felt like its entire contents into the bowl.

The faint smell of pizza and liquor reached my nose, causing me to lean over once more and I managed to expel more of my stomach's contents.

Ten minutes later, I finally stood up. I flushed the toilet and washed my face. There was a soft knock on the door.

It was Ricky's voice. "Hey, are you okay in there?"

"Yea," I muttered. "I'll be out in a minute."

When I opened the door, Ricky was standing there looking at me innocently. "Everything okay?" he asked.

"Yea," I said. "I'm not sure what was in that bottle, but it didn't agree with my stomach at all."

He smiled at me. "Was that your first time drinking alcohol?"

"Well, yea. My parents would kill me if they knew I drank that."

"Mine would too, silly," he said. "Why do you think we did that in secret? But if it's your first time, then that explains why it made you sick. It will be better next time."

There was going to be a next time? The revelation that Ricky drank alcohol before shocked me. I didn't say anything in response and just walked past him. In the living room, the other boys were running around, wearing nothing but their underwear or boxer shorts.

I found a quiet place in the corner and laid down. I still wasn't feeling well and wasn't in the mood for their horseplay. I didn't even bother to change. I was still wearing my jeans and shirt, but I didn't care. I just wanted to sleep.

Something woke me up. I looked around. The lights had been turned off and I could see the lumps that were the bodies of all the boys asleep on the living room floor. What was it that woke me up? I glanced at my watch. It was only 2:10 AM.

I turned back over to sleep, and I felt something again. I turned over and saw Ricky lying beside me. His eyes seemed to be closed, but his hand had found its way under my shirt and was resting on my chest. It was warm and gave me a nice feeling. I brought my hand up to meet his and kept it there for a while. It made me feel safe and relaxed. I sat up and looked down at him. I could see that he was wearing nothing but his underwear. I ran my hand down the length of his back and stopped right above his buttocks.

In the back of my mind, I could still hear Ms. Anderson from this morning talking about remaining pure and abstaining from all appearances of evil and sexual impurity.

Were these thoughts included in that? Would I go to hell for having these thoughts? I shook my head. I didn't want to think about that.

I brought my hand a little further down, and let it rest on his underwear. In the dark, I could make out the shape and feel of his butt. Again, those words from Ms. Anderson came floating back to me, and I retracted my hand. *Was I a sinner who was going to go to hell?*

I looked up at the ceiling for a few minutes as I thought these things over. It occurred to me that my school couldn't be right about everything. *Could they?*

Ricky wasn't just my friend, he was my boyfriend, and there wasn't anything that they could say that could change it. I pulled my shirt over my head and tossed it into the corner, followed by my jeans. Now I was only in my underwear as well.

I scooted right up against him, and I put my arms around him. He murmured something in his sleep and opened his arms to embrace me as well. This was how I fell asleep.

When I opened my eyes again, it was bright out. I checked my watch. It was 9:30 AM. I looked around me. Everyone was still sound asleep. Some noise in the kitchen drew my attention. It was Mrs. Vergara, shuffling around, and making breakfast. The succulent smell of pancakes reached my nostrils.

I suddenly felt very self-conscious. I looked around for my clothes and Mrs. Vergara noticed I was awake.

"Good morning, dear," she said to me.

"Good morning," I muttered back, still red from embarrassment as I kept the blankets wrapped around myself. I grabbed my clothes and awkwardly pulled my jeans back on while still under the blankets. I then stood up and pulled my shirt over my head.

"Is it okay if I take a shower?" I asked her.

"Of course, it is, dear," she replied. I first went to Ricky's room, got out my clothes, and then proceeded to the bathroom, where I took a hot shower.

The water felt great on my body, but I still felt a little nauseous. I tried to shake it off. I still didn't know what was in that bottle, but one thing was for sure. I wouldn't be drinking it again soon, whatever it was.

I returned to the kitchen and saw that Mrs. Vergara was setting out plates and cutlery on the table. "Honey," she said to me. "We were thinking of going to the city after we eat. Would you like to come with us?"

"Sure," I said. "But what about my mom?"

"When did she say that she'd pick you up again?" she asked me.

"I don't know," I replied. "Sometime this evening I guess."

"It's settled," Mrs. Vergara said. "We'll leave soon and come back before dinner."

"Okay," I said with a smile on my face. This was going to be another great day.

It was almost 10:00 AM by the time everyone else was up. They would have slept longer, but Mrs. Vergara went and shook them all awake. Wiping the sleep from their eyes, they joined us at the table. We ate, everyone showered, and we took off for the city. Austin and Eddy had to go home, so it was just Ricky, Carlos, Albert, and me. Their eyes showed they were hungover, but Mrs. Vergara didn't seem to have noticed.

Just like the last time I stayed with the Vergaras', we went to the mall, which was one of the biggest in the country. I followed the boys to the arcade. I'd never been in there before and as soon as I entered, I realized why I wasn't allowed in there.

After I got over the noise and the visual stimulation, I saw that most of the games were gory and violent. There was a first-person shooter game, and another where you aimed to shoot zombies in the head. I wasn't sure what to think initially, but the boys seemed to get pretty excited.

"Let's do that one first!" Carlos yelled as they ran over to one corner. It was a two-person game where you helped the other to kill these big man-eating slugs.

"What about you?" I asked Ricky. "What game do you want to play?"

"Just wait," he said. "Let me play this with Carlos first, and then we can go play something else."

I stepped back and waited for them to finish their game. I glanced around and even I felt a little uncomfortable at some of these games. Nothing but blood, guts, and gore.

I often complained about how conservative my parents were, but I wasn't prepared for what I saw here either. Even in the anime I watched, I never saw anything this brutal and violent. I just stood there awkwardly as the other boys kept playing. It surprised me how enthusiastic Ricky was with this kind of thing, as well. I still wasn't sure what to think of this new side of him.

After about ten minutes, Ricky was by my side again as the other boys continued playing. "What do you want to do?" he asked me.

"How about that?" I said and pointed to a game in the corner. It had a small basketball hoop. The point was to throw these small balls and you would get points for every time they went into the net.

"Naw, I have a better idea," he said. "Here, come with me."

He took me by the hand and led me to a corner where there weren't many people. "Here," he said. "Let's try this one."

I looked and saw a game with images from a fantasy anime that we both liked. This was more my style. Ricky inserted a couple of game tokens, and we played.

Never mind this being my first time at an arcade, this was my first time playing any sort of video game. Ever. I couldn't believe what I had been missing out on. It was so much fun, and I found I was pretty good at it too.

We played three rounds before we found something else to play. "Come here," Ricky said with a twinkle in his eye, and I followed him to an even more secluded corner.

"What are we doing here?" I asked, and the words were barely out of my lips before he jumped on me. I accepted his mouth willingly as I put my hand around the back of his head to pull him in.

When we broke apart, I looked him in the eyes and realized just how lucky I was to have someone like him in my life. Seeing him only a couple times a week just wasn't enough, but at least we've had plenty of time this weekend.

"I love you," he said to him.

"I love you too," he replied, and he leaned in for another kiss.

"What are you guys doing over here?"

We both spun around to see Carlos and Albert standing there, staring at us with suspicion.

CHAPTER 4

As a kid, some of my most memorable moments were when I would spend a weekend at my grandma and grandpa's house, or as we affectionately called them, Oma and Opa.

It was a tradition that we would stay with them in December before Christmas. We would help Oma make shortbread cookies and other treats for the holidays.

I had five younger siblings and a handful of cousins, and so we'd take turns and go at different times. Me being the oldest, I got to go first and would often share that weekend with my cousin, Peter, who was the same age as me.

These were some of the fondest memories that I have from my childhood, but one time sticks out more than any other. It was over a year earlier. I was thirteen, almost fourteen. I had been studying Dutch for some time already, as both my grandparents were Dutch immigrants, and so staying with them provided ample opportunity to improve my language skills.

I just started my anime craze at the time too and started studying Japanese. My grandparents thought I should focus more on my Dutch before taking up another language, so I left my study book at home during this visit.

My grandparents lived on a dairy farm fifteen minutes out of town, and it was always a treat when we got to spend some time with them. Oma was one of the sweetest people you could ever meet. Opa was much quieter and more subdued, but he was a hard worker and had a lot of patience. I couldn't remember a time where I ever saw him get angry or raise his voice.

Today, my mom took me there after school on Friday afternoon, and I stayed until Sunday morning.

Peter was there already with his mom, my Aunt Sarah. She was by far my favorite aunty. She was my mom's sister and also a Christian, but she wasn't as conservative as my parents were.

The same went for my grandparents, oddly enough. The rest of the family attended a different church on the other side of town. They thought the one we went to was too conservative, so spending time with my extended family gave me more freedom than I had at home.

Peter and I shared the guest room, which had a queen-sized bed. I put my things in there and we had a quick snack before the two of us went outside to help Opa milk cows. I always enjoyed helping around the farm and milking the cows was one of my favorite activities.

The barn where the milking took place was just across the farmyard. Opa didn't have a large operation. He had about fifty cows that he milked twice a day. Opa did most of the milking, although, as I was getting older, he gave me more responsibility. This time, Peter and I helped herd the cows into the milking parlor. We fed the newborn calves in the adjoining building and then cleaned up after the milking was finished.

Everything took about two hours from start to finish. Finally, we were sitting around the dinner table. Oma made stamppot, a Dutch dish made of mashed potatoes, carrots, and cut up pieces of sausage. It was one of my favorites and vanilla vla followed for dessert.

Peter brought over a DVD. It was the new Pokémon movie that came out recently and I hadn't seen it yet. It was banned in my house, so when I was with Peter, it was always a chance to catch up on some of these shows and movies I wasn't able to watch otherwise.

The next morning, we didn't help with the milking as we would bake cookies with Oma, so we didn't have to get up as early.

We helped clean up after dinner and then watched the movie. It was about 10:00 PM by the time we climbed into bed. At home, I had my own bedroom, but here I shared a bed with Peter. I wasn't used to that, but I could bear it if it was only for a couple of days. I was often nervous sleeping away from home anyway, so I found it comforting.

"Tomorrow we're going to go swimming in town," Peter said to me. "Do you want to join us?"

"Sure," I said. "But I thought we were helping Oma bake cookies."

He rolled his eyes at me. "That's in the morning silly."

"Oh," I said.

"We'll go in the afternoon. Before dinner."

"Okay, sure," I said. "I didn't bring my swim trunks. My parents won't be happy if I go to a public swim."

"You can borrow a pair of mine," Peter said. "And don't worry about your parents. We won't tell them."

"Okay," I said and I rolled over.

I woke up with a start. I looked around and saw it was still dark outside. I checked my watch and saw that it was only 2:00 AM. It was still early, but this usually happened when I slept away from home. I often had a hard time sleeping in a new place. I looked over at Peter. He was sleeping soundly.

Oma was nice enough to leave one of the hallway lights on so I could find my way to the bathroom. I crept along slowly. I saw shadows around every corner, but taking a deep breath of courage, I dashed to the door, locking it behind me.

I used to be scared of the dark when I was younger. I was getting over it, but it was harder when I was away from home. I did my business and then stuck my head out of the bathroom door again. I closed my eyes, said a silent prayer, and then I made a run for it. I pushed the bedroom door open and ducked underneath the covers.

I looked back over at Peter. He stirred for a moment, rolled over, and began softly snoring. I lay back down and waited for my heart to stop racing before I fell back to sleep.

We both woke up at 8:00 AM and got dressed. Oma made a scrumptious breakfast of pancakes and bacon. I loved how she always took the time to prepare such nice meals. I smelled something else in the air as well.

"Did you start baking without us?" I asked.

She just smiled at me as she set her coffee mug down. I recognized the aroma of her almond creamer. "I just put in a tray of blueberry muffins," she said. "But don't worry. There's still plenty of work for us to do."

"Okay," I said as I eagerly ate my food. Christmas was only three weeks away and my oma was already busy preparing all kinds of baked goods for our family gathering.

After we finished eating, we cleared the table and started baking. Oma turned on the radio and put on some Christian Christmas music.

By the time Opa came back inside from his work, the whole house smelled like a bakery. We made an assortment of items, including shortbread cookies, gingerbread men, and cinnamon buns. We were even allowed a sample before lunch.

My mom never had time to teach me how to bake and so this was the highlight of the year.

After lunch, Aunt Sarah showed up and took Peter and me into town for the afternoon. The two of us sat in the back seat and my aunt turned to talk to us.

"So, Jeremiah, how's everything been? Are you okay?"

"Yea," I replied. "Everything's going well."

"Perfect," she said. "How about school? Is that going alright too?"

"Yea," I said. "It's going."

"I hope I'm not talking out of place, but have you ever considered going to the public school?"

I thought for a moment before replying. "I would like to, but my parents won't let me. I've already asked them."

"Oh, really?" she said. "That's too bad. You and Peter get along so well, it would be nice if you could go to school together."

"I know," I sighed. "Trust me, we've talked about it many times, but they won't budge."

"I see," she said. "It's okay, don't worry about it. Maybe they'll change later. You never know, right?"

"Yea," I muttered as I looked out the window at the snow-covered fields passing by.

We arrived at our local pool, and I was both excited and anxious. I had only been allowed to go swimming with other church families. This was my first time going to a regular public swim.

Peter met up with a couple of his friends and they introduced themselves to me, but I quickly forgot their names. A thought distracted me. The church families that I swam with were taught to be as private about their bodies as I was, so everyone changed their clothes in the stalls, and no one thought anything of it.

But from my experience at summer camp, I realized many less conservative kids weren't shy about nudity and would change in front of each other. *Would that be the same in this case?* I was too shy to change in front of others, but it made it even worse when I was the only one to go hide in the stalls.

Sure enough, Peter and his two friends both started stripping before even locating a locker to put their things in. I tried to ignore them as I put my bag into an empty locker. I pulled out the swimming trunks I borrowed from Peter, and I quickly located a stall to change in.

When I emerged, I saw I was alone in the change room. I shrugged, put my items back in my locker, and headed out to the pool.

Peter and his friends were already in the water, horsing around and playing rough. I looked around and saw that it wasn't very crowded, despite it being a Saturday afternoon.

Not sure what to do, and not really knowing anyone else, I crossed my arms and headed over to the hot tub. A rubber ball came flying and narrowly missed me. I turned to the pool to look at the boys.

"Hey," Peter called out to me. "Come play water polo with us."

I hesitated. "Um, just wait. Maybe later," I said and made a beeline to the hot tub. As much as I liked swimming, I had bad social anxiety and had a hard time in social situations I wasn't accustomed to.

I stepped into the tub, and it took me about five minutes to get used to the hot water until I could fully submerge myself. As I sat there, I observed my surroundings. I realized why my parents only ever let me go to the pool with other church families.

Most of the girls wore two-piece swimsuits, which only covered the bare minimum. This was my first time seeing something like this since looking at a dirty magazine one boy brought to summer camp the year before.

Not just the older ones, but some younger girls as well. A couple of them were as young as my sisters. My mom would have a fit if they even suggested wearing something like that.

I shuddered and brought my eyes back to the tub that I was sitting in. It was large and there were only two other people in there with me. A couple of older men. One of them was so relaxed he looked like he was about to pass out.

I surveyed the area again, and I saw the boys, way over in the big pool, jumping around and throwing a ball at each other. Something occurred to me at that moment. One of Peter's friends was quite cute. I couldn't recall his name, but I thought it was something like Scott. Yea, that sounded right.

As they played, I continued to watch him. Scott. He had short blonde hair and was tall for his age. Then again, so was I. I estimated him to be about the same height as myself. His body was smooth, and his stomach was nicely toned, with just a tiny trace amount of hair around his lower abdomen.

As far as I could remember, this was only the second time that I had looked at another boy with any sort of interest or sense of attraction. The first time was at summer camp last year. I didn't go back since that time due to something that happened there, but there was this boy named Daniel I was drawn to. We had become close friends, but nothing more emerged from our friendship. He chased around other girls and I knew that my attraction to him wasn't reciprocated.

I was also confused about what to make of these thoughts. I knew I couldn't be gay, so what was it? Just a light attraction, I suppose?

I let out an audible sigh as I watched the boys playing in the water. I wanted to go join them, but I would have to get over my anxiety first. I noticed a couple of other people entering the hot tub. I scooted over to make some room and noticed they were both young. Only a couple of years older than me. Maybe fifteen or sixteen?

It was a boy and a girl, and they seemed to be a couple. The girl was wearing a small bikini, and the boy had his arms wrapped around her. They were both giggling. As she complained that the water was too hot, he leaned in and gave her a kiss on the mouth.

I felt awkward seeing this and diverted my eyes. This was something only permitted between married people. These two teens were clearly fornicating with each other. Something that was sinful.

I waited about thirty seconds, then I looked up to see that they were still at it, so I pulled myself up and climbed out of the hot tub.

I walked around the side of the pool, not sure what to do or say, but then Peter caught my eye and he waved me over to him. I took the plunge and hopped into the pool.

"What are you guys doing?" I asked.

"We're playing *piggy in the middle*," Peter said. "Are you in?"

"Yea, sure," I replied.

"Okay, you're the piggy!" Peter shouted, and they all pushed off to make more space between them and me.

They started tossing the ball around and I tried to catch it. Before long, I brushed up against Scott. He had his back to me, and I reached around to get the ball from him. As we wrestled in the water for a few moments, my hand brushed against the front of his trunks, and I felt something hard. Immediately, I froze and pulled my hands back.

"Got it!" Scott yelled as he took advantage of my distraction and tossed the ball to the other boys. It took me a moment to recover, and I was back in the game.

I went back to the changing room earlier than the others. I was tired and ready to go home. I grabbed my clothes and found an empty stall, which was easy, as there wasn't anyone else in the changing room.

I dried off and was just about to pull my trunks down when I noticed a shadow on the other side of the curtain. I pulled it back, and I saw Scott there, smiling as he stared back at me.

"Hey," he said through his broad grin. He then stepped in, forcing me to back up to give him some room.

"What's up?" I asked. I could feel my voice quivering.

"You noticed something in my trunks, didn't you?" he asked me.

"What? Um, no," I said awkwardly.

"Don't lie," he said to me. "I already saw you checking me out. To be honest, it kind of turned me on."

I didn't know what that meant, but I looked at the ground as my face heated up.

"You're cute," he said to me. I didn't know how to respond, and I continued to stare at the ground. "I'll show you if you show me," he continued. That took me by surprise, and I wasn't even sure that I heard him right.

"What?" I said in surprise. "Show what?"

"You know," he said. "That," and his eyes darted down to my groin for a fleeting moment.

My heart was beating hard in my chest as I stood there, not sure how to respond. "Here, I'll go first," he said, and without even hesitating, he dropped his trunks down to his ankles.

My eyes opened wide in shock. I hadn't seen many of those in my life, but I knew right away that it didn't look at all like my own. The head was covered by skin that I didn't have. I suddenly felt even more self-conscious than I had ten seconds earlier.

"You like it?" he asked with a mischievous grin.

"It's alright," I said in a small voice.

"Now it's your turn," he said. He still hadn't pulled his trunks back up. "Hurry, before someone comes."

I took a deep breath and placed my fingers in the waistband of my trunks, and looked back at him. He was still smiling.

"It's okay," he said. "Hurry it up. The others will be here soon."

I nodded unenthusiastically, and I pulled them down. Not far. Just enough for my penis to be visible. He saw it and started laughing.

I was confused. I knew it didn't look the same as his, but I didn't know why that made it so funny. "What's wrong?" I asked.

"What happened to it?" he said. "Why does it look so weird? You don't have any foreskin!"

I felt red in the face. "I-I don't know," I stammered. "I thought it's normal."

"Well, it's not," he said. I wished that smirk on his face would disappear. I pulled my trunks back up, grabbed my clothes, and went to a stall on the other side of the change room. My cheeks were burning up by this point, and I had to calm down before I could change into my clothes.

I still wasn't exactly sure what happened, but it affected me somehow. I felt emotions and feelings I never experienced before. I also felt shame and embarrassment.

That was how I had my first ever sexual experience.

After I dressed, I left the changing room, and I saw my Aunt Sarah standing outside waiting for us. Peter came out about fifteen minutes later. He said goodbye to his friends, and we climbed back into the car.

"Are we going back to Oma's house now?" I asked.

"We want to make one stop first," Peter said, as he turned to look at me. "I want to pick up a couple more packs of Pokémon cards."

"Really?" I asked. I couldn't believe my luck. I had always wanted to start collecting the cards again, but my parents wouldn't let me. I had been given some as a gift before and I kept them a secret from my parents. I ended up getting caught with them at school. My parents were furious when they found out and grounded me for a month. That was the punishment for playing with something that was of the devil.

We entered the small sports' and novelty shop and I walked with Peter up to the counter where there was a display case of the cards that we were looking for.

"Are you going to buy some too?" Peter asked.

"I don't know," I said with apprehension. "I'm not allowed to have them. My mom said that they're occultic."

"No, they aren't," he scoffed. "Here, I'll buy you a pack."

"No, it's okay," I said. "I have my own money. I'm just wondering if I dare to do it or not."

"Just do it," he pressed. "If your mom gets mad, then just leave them at my house and you can play with me when we hang out."

I thought about that for a moment and the idea seemed sensible, so I pulled out a five-dollar bill from my pocket and placed it on the counter I took the pack that was nearest to me.

Back at our grandparent's house, I couldn't wait to open my pack of cards. I couldn't believe my luck. I opened the package and held up the cards as if they were some sort of precious metal.

"Pretty cool, huh?" Peter said to me.

"Boys, dinnertime!" Oma called us.

"Let's play when we get back," Peter said, and we rushed to go eat. This would be our last night on the farm.

This time dinner was split-pea soup, another one of my favorites, and we both helped ourselves to second servings. Our grandparents also took the opportunity to ask about our home lives. Especially me. Sometimes I had the feeling that they didn't approve of how my parents were raising us.

"So how are things at your church?" Oma asked as she was getting out her Bible. It was a tradition at their house to do a Bible reading after dinner every night. Everyone in my family, except my parents, my siblings and me, went to a more progressive-minded church on the other side of town. My parents considered that church to be too liberal and not theologically sound. My grandparents and the rest of the family thought that our church was too conservative and fundamentalist. My mom hadn't been so conservative until she met my dad. That was something I had sussed out on my own, and it aggravated me.

"Everything's okay," I said. "Just normal I guess."

"How are you liking your school?" she asked. Aunt Sarah had asked the same thing. They obviously didn't approve of us going there. Neither did I, for that matter, but try telling that to my parents.

Opa took the Bible from her and opened it up. What was interesting to note was that unlike at my home, here they read the Bible in the New International Version, or NIV. Not the old-fashioned KJV, which was the only one that I was allowed to read.

After we read the Bible and had devotions, Peter and I took a quick shower and then hurried to the bedroom, where we played Pokémon until late at night. Finally, at around 10:30 PM, Oma knocked on our door and told us to go to sleep.

The next morning, we got up early and got dressed. It was Sunday morning. I'd go back home after church, but first I had the privilege of going to church with my grandparents. What fascinated me the most about their church was that it had a worship band. My church didn't agree with worship music, and so they limited us to singing old hymns.

The congregation was also much younger than I was used to. There were many more young families and kids my age as well. I sat with my grandparents and Peter. His parents joined us shortly after the service started.

It was the most interesting church service that I witnessed up to that moment. Not just the worship team, but how enthusiastic and friendlier the congregants were. At my church, everyone was so stiff and formal. And then there was the Bible Reading. This was my first time at a church where they didn't read the KJV.

Once the service was over, I hung out with Peter and a couple of his friends. They also had Pokémon cards, so, while the adults were having coffee, we found a quiet corner in the sanctuary where we played.

My mom showed up shortly after to pick me up. I couldn't push the cards out of sight before she noticed. The look on her face said it all. She didn't say anything at that moment though, and I thought maybe I wouldn't get into trouble. I was wrong.

We barely arrived home when she turned on me. "Give me those cards," she barked. "Where did you get them from?"

"I bought them," I said. "With my money."

"Where?" she demanded. "You were baking cookies with Oma."

"I went with Peter and Aunt Sarah," I replied. "We went swimming and then they took me to the store."

"You went swimming?" she said. "Where?"

I backed up. I hadn't ever seen her this angry before. "In town," I replied.

"Oh, dear Lord," she hissed. "I've told you, that you're only to go there if we go together as a family. Not by yourself."

"What does it matter?" I retorted. "I had fun, and that's all that should matter. You never let us do anything to have fun!" Tears were streaming down my face at this point.

"That's bull and you know it," she said. "We want you to have fun, but we want you to be safe. Your father and I need to approve of these activities first."

"Why?" I said. "We went swimming. What's the harm?"

"What's the harm?" she repeated back. "Do you realize the temptations that are out there? You're becoming a teenager, Jeremiah, and I'm just trying to protect you."

"Well, I don't need protecting," I said. "I just want to go out and have fun. All you want us to do is go to church and school and that's it."

The slap across my face stung. I brought my hand up to feel my cheek. It was warm to the touch.

"That's not true!" my mom said. Her face was beet red. "And that's enough. Give me those cards."

"No," I said. "They're mine. I paid for them with *my* money."

"Give them here!" she snarled. She forcefully grabbed me by my jacket, reached into my pocket, and pulled them out.

"These are going in the trash," she said.

"No!" I yelled back. "Mom, you can't do this. Those are mine! I paid for them!"

She slapped me again. Harder this time. I could feel a small welt forming.

"I have warned you many times about playing with magic and the devil," she said, her voice getting louder. "Go to your room!

Now!" I stood firm as I wiped away my tears. I held one hand to my cheek. The pain was getting worse.

"I said now!" she yelled at the top of her lungs, which almost caused me to stumble backward.

I turned around, ran into my room, and slammed the door as hard as I could. I threw myself onto my bed and sobbed into my pillow.

"*It wasn't fair,*" I thought to myself. "*She won't let me do anything. Just go to church and that's it. That's all our life revolves around.*"

It was at that moment that I realized the importance of keeping my interests quiet. All of my interests, be it movies, books, or games. That was the day I started keeping secrets.

CHAPTER 5

No one said a word on the drive back home. I couldn't be sure if the boys actually saw us kiss or not. But they seemed to have sussed something out, judging by the looks and awkward silence they gave us.

Mrs. Vergara didn't seem to have noticed that anything was off, and she tried to ask us how our day was. When she didn't get much of an answer back, she must have assumed that we were just tired. She turned on the radio and continued driving.

The atmosphere didn't change much when we got home, either. Carlos and Albert were still acting strange by the time they left, even though they never said anything about it.

I sat with Ricky in his room while I waited for my mom to pick me up. "Do you think they saw us?" I asked him.

He just shrugged. "I don't know. Maybe."

"I hope they don't say anything to anybody," I said. "I knew it was a bad idea to do that there."

He shrugged again. I didn't like how nonchalant he was being about this.

"Don't you care if anyone finds out?" I asked him.

"Sure, I do," he said. "But they're my friends. I'm sure everything will be cool."

"I hope so," I said. I wasn't as confident as he was.

"Come here," he said to me, and he drew me in for a long kiss. After we broke apart, there was a soft knock on the door and his mom stuck her head in.

"Jeremiah dear, your mom's here," she said.

"Oh, okay," I said. "Thank you." I turned to look at Ricky. "See you around," I said to him. He gave me a fist bump, then I grabbed my bag and ran out to my mom's van.

It was a few days later, and I was sitting in my bedroom doing my homework when my mom called out to me.

"Jeremiah, phone for you!"

I usually didn't get phone calls, but I went out and took the phone from her. "Hello?" I said.

"Hi," came the reply. It was Ricky.

"Hi," I said. "What's up?

"Just wanted to let you know I talked with Carlos and Albert."

"Okay..." I could hear my heart beating in my ears. "What did they say?" I asked.

"Well... they saw us kiss." At hearing this, my heart dropped to the floor, leaving a dull pain in my chest.

"Really?" I said. My voice was shaking. "So now what?"

There was a pause before he spoke again. "At first, they were disgusted, but they said that they won't tell anyone, as long as I don't hit on them or anything."

"Oh?" was all that I could say. I felt numb. Numb and scared.

"Yea, it'll be fine," Ricky said to me. "Try not to stress about it. I just thought you should know."

But I did stress about it. If my parents, or anyone at the church, ever caught wind of that, it would be my end. I couldn't let that happen.

"You're sure they won't tell anyone?" I asked.

"I'm positive," he said. "It'll be okay. Trust me."

"Alright," I said. "But we have to be more careful. No taking chances like that anymore. Okay?"

"Agreed," he said, and that was it. I went to bed full of apprehension about what the future would bring, but over the following days and weeks, nothing happened, so I pushed that incident to the back of my mind.

It was May 15th, and I woke up for church as normal. It surprised me to see both my parents were gone. I ran to look outside, but the van was missing from the driveway. I scratched my head. Something felt strange.

I walked back into the house and there I saw a note on the kitchen table. I picked it up to read it. It was from my dad.

Jeremiah, your mom is having the baby. There won't be any church today. Take care of the kids and help them with breakfast. I will be home later today. Love, Dad.

I put the note down and looked around. A couple of the kids were already up and active. I let out a groan as I went and helped them with breakfast.

My dad came home around lunchtime. My brothers and sisters were eating grilled cheese sandwiches I made for them while I snuck in some anime. I turned the TV off just as he came in the door.

"Hey you guys," he said. "Your mom had a healthy baby girl. Her name is Olivia, and she is doing really well. Do you all want to go see her?"

All the other kids jumped up and down enthusiastically, so fifteen minutes later, they were all piling into the van.

"Is it okay if I stay home?" I asked my dad. "I'm tired and not feeling well."

"Yea, that's fine," my dad said. "We'll be home soon."

I watched them pull out of the driveway, and then I turned the TV back on to watch my show. I watched until the phone rang, making me jump. It must have been about twenty minutes later. I lifted the phone off of the receiver.

"Hello?" I said.

"Hey," said Ricky. "How are you? You weren't at church today."

"Yea," I said. "My mom had the baby. Dad took her to the hospital, so we stayed home.

"Oh, I see," he said. "Where are you now? Still at home?"

"Yea," I said. "Why? What's up?"

"I'm just bored is all," he said. "I was going to ask you to come over."

"I wish I could," I said. "I miss you."

"I miss you too," he said. "Hey, were you going to go to the youth convention next week?

"Oh, I almost forgot about that. My parents said maybe. I'll ask them again."

"Just tell them you're going with me," Ricky said. "I'm sure it'll be fine."

"Okay, I'll talk to my dad when he gets home," I said, and I hung up.

I almost forgot about that. Some members of our church were going into the city for a large Christian youth convention being organized by another of the many churches in our town.

It was going to be a three-day event full of Christian worship bands and speakers. My parents didn't like modern music. They thought it was one of many examples of the church getting corrupted by the secular world, but this was one of the biggest Christian conventions in the world and there would be lots of speakers and evangelists there, including a couple that my parents revered.

That night, my dad ordered pizza before going to work and I was left to babysit. My mom came back from the hospital on Tuesday, and I got to hold my new baby sister for the first time. She was cute and adorable, but it also meant that once my mom went back to work, I'd have another kid to change diapers for.

My parents ended up allowing me to go to the youth conference with Ricky after all, so on Friday after school, Mrs. Vergara picked me up and took us to the church where the meeting point was.

There were twenty-two teenagers in total and four chaperones. Two men and two women. They were all young and seemed to be friendly and full of energy. It was differed from what I was used to at my church.

We drove straight to the city where we parked at a local church that was going to host us for the weekend. We were directed to our sleeping quarters. One big room for the boys and one for the girls. I looked at the mostly empty room. It appeared to be a Sunday School classroom.

We laid out our sleeping bags on the floor, and then went back to the bus and headed to the conference. The first session was going to begin soon.

The conference was held in a massive arena that was normally used for hockey games or rock concerts. Capacity was eighteen thousand people. I had never been in such a place before. I was in awe as we walked through the entrance and past the ticket agents.

The energy was something else. I was so mesmerized by everything I saw as we made our way through the crowd to find our seats. The conference kicked off with a firework display followed by an opening speech by the organizers, and then a Christian rock band came out. The music was so loud that the floor was vibrating under my feet. It was surreal.

While I was listening, I made a realization. For the first time, I appreciated that there could be Christian rock bands. My whole life I had been told that loud music, especially rock, was the work of the devil, and yet here was a Christian band playing rock music, but with lyrics that praised the Lord. I wasn't sure what to make of it, but I thought it was something incredible.

I was exhausted by the time we made it back to the church that evening. I fell down on my bedding and I was prepared to fall asleep without even changing. Ricky pulled his bedding over beside me and we found a quiet corner away from everyone else.

We got up and went looking for the bathroom to brush our teeth. This was the biggest church that I had ever been in, and it would be easy to get lost in. As we were looking around, Ricky reached around and grabbed my butt. I swatted his hand away.

"Shh, not here," I whispered to him. "Someone will see." I knew he was trying to be playful, but it put me on edge.

He reached out and grabbed my arm, and we both stopped. There wasn't anyone around us and so he came forward and we made out. As much as I enjoyed it, I got a pang of guilt in my chest and I pushed him away.

"Not here," I said. "We're in a church."

"So?"

"So... it doesn't feel right," I said.

"You don't think that God likes love?" he asked in a joking tone, and he came towards me again, but I held out my hands.

"No, seriously," I said firmly. "What if someone sees us?"

"Who?" he asked. "There's no one here."

"That's beside the point," I said. "I just don't feel comfortable doing that here."

"Come on," he said. "Just a couple of minutes."

Just as he leaned in again, I spotted it. An illuminated sign that read: *Restrooms*.

"Hey, look," I said, interrupting him. "The bathrooms are over there. Come on." I ran down the hall in that direction, with Ricky trailing behind me.

The bathrooms were much bigger than at our church. There were six toilet stalls, just as many sinks, and a couple of shower stalls in the corner. It was almost as big as the changing room at our local swimming pool. I was amazed.

"No one's here either," Ricky pointed out.

I looked at him and thought for a moment. "Okay," I relented. "Let's make it quick," and I moved towards him. Our lips barely touched when a sound outside made us jump and we quickly turned to the sink.

We listened for a moment, but no one came in. My heart raced as I pulled out my toothbrush. I looked over at Ricky, and he appeared much calmer than me. I always envied him for his calm demeanor.

We brushed our teeth and washed our faces. I decided that showering could wait until the morning. We were glad to have discovered the illuminated signs hanging from the ceiling and we used them to get back to our sleeping quarters.

Pretty much everyone was lying on the floor and ready to sleep. I couldn't blame them. I felt exhausted too. I went over to the corner and climbed into my sleeping bag, with Ricky at my side.

Soon the lights went out. I reached out and felt Ricky's hand in the dark. It was warm to the touch, and it gave me a feeling of comfort. He gave me a firm squeeze and scooted a little closer to me. I found his face and gave him a light peck on his cheek. "I love you," I whispered, as loud as I dared.

"I love you too," he said. "Thanks for coming with me."

I smiled. "Good night," I said to him.

"Good night," he replied, and I drifted off to sleep, with my hand still in his grip.

The next morning, we were woken up at 6:00 AM. I squinted as my eyes adjusted to the flood of bright light. All around me, everyone was up and pulling on their clothes. I looked over at Ricky, but he wasn't there. I assumed he went ahead of me and so I grabbed my bag and headed to the bathroom.

It looked like I was the first one there, but then I heard the shower running. In a low voice, I said, "Hello, is anyone here?"

Ricky stuck his head out of the showers, smiling.

"Good morning, sweetheart," he said in a sing-song voice.

"Good morning, to you too," I replied. "You're up early."

"I couldn't sleep," he said. "You want to join me?"

I laughed out loud. "You really are a brazen one, aren't you?" I said to him as I selected the free stall next to his. I showered as quickly as I could. I was excited. It was going to be another full day, with Ricky by my side, and no parents.

Sure, there were the chaperones and other kids, but they didn't know us the same way, nor were they as strict as my parents were. They afforded us much more freedom than I was used to.

It was a busy day. The first session started at 8:00 AM. We went for lunch at 11:30 AM, followed by the various breakout sessions After the morning concert, we could wander around by ourselves. There was a complex across the street that held the afternoon breakout sessions. Everyone could go there in their own friend groups, as long as we met at the rendezvous point at 4:00 PM, where we would then go to the arena for the evening session.

Ricky and I both had pocket money from our parents. I had one hundred dollars. Ricky had twice that. The money was to buy meals and snacks, with some to spare for buying souvenirs.

We ate pizza in the food court, and then we headed down to the vendors' hall to buy some merchandise. A hundred dollars wasn't a lot for the weekend, but I could spare enough to buy a CD from one band I saw perform. Ricky bought a different CD from the same band, as well as a T-shirt for both him and myself. This was so cool. It felt like we were out on a date. A proper date, despite the discretion that we were forced to practice. The final worship concert of the day started at 5:00 PM and then we headed back to the church.

It was almost 9:00 PM by the time we were back, and I was completely exhausted. I couldn't even be bothered to change clothes, but Ricky coaxed me into getting up and going to take a shower.

By the time we went to the bathroom, we were the last ones to use it, so we had it all to ourselves. We brushed our teeth and headed for the shower. Before I could get into a stall, Ricky grabbed me, leaned in, and kissed me. At first, I accepted him, but after a few seconds, I pulled back and put my finger to his lip, as if to shush him.

"Not here," I said. "Not now."

"Why not?" he asked.

"I just... feel nervous is all."

"Feel nervous?" he said with a low chuckle. "There's no one here."

He tried to come in again, but I put my hand on his chest to stop him. "Not at the church, okay? Let's wait until we're back home."

His eyes looked down and right away I knew I hurt him, but at that moment I couldn't be bothered about it. I wasn't in the mood, and I stepped into an empty shower stall without waiting for him to say anything.

I was halfway through when I heard him leave. I let out a sigh. I was feeling so many emotions. I was tired and ready to go home. I was glad to have him by my side, but he was being pushy, and I just couldn't stand the thought of us getting caught again. It was bad enough that his friends saw us, but what if it was one of these church kids? The thought of someone discovering us made my heart race. We lived in a small town. What if word reached my parents? I couldn't let that happen.

When I went to bed, Ricky was already there. He had his back turned to me and seemed to be sound asleep. I laid down beside him and once the lights were out, I reached out to touch him, but he didn't react at all, and so I rolled over and went to sleep.

Sunday was our final day, and it started off as normal. Well, almost normal. Ricky wouldn't speak to me, and he barely even looked at him. I went to the bathroom alone to freshen up. He had finished already, so there was no point in asking him to come with me.

On the way back, I dragged my feet along the carpet. My heart felt so heavy. I didn't mean to upset or hurt him. He was just being more open than I was prepared to be, and it freaked me out. I was scared.

I put my things back in my bag and glanced at Ricky. He sat in the corner, reading a book, and didn't even acknowledge me. I let out a sigh and just looked out the window. I didn't know what I should do. It was my first time being in a relationship. *Is this what it felt like to get into a fight?*

After a quick bite, we piled into the bus and headed back to the arena, where we enjoyed an uplifting morning worship service. It was the afternoon event where I felt even more uneasy, if that was possible.

The speaker was an older man. I guessed him to be in his mid to late fifties. He was a pastor from Texas who ministered in San Francisco and his topic was on homosexuality.

"I've lived and worked in San Francisco for many years," he said. "You know, that city has been called the 'gay capital of the world' and in many ways that's true."

He had my attention. I was hooked on every word, even though I wasn't enjoying it. It made me more miserable.

"First off, I want to preface this by saying that I don't hate homosexuals. I love homosexuals. I just want to warn them of their sin, so that they can avoid eternal damnation."

He paused, almost as if for dramatic effect. "We are surrounded by a culture that tells our young people that it's okay to be gay. That is one of the biggest lies of this decade, boys and girls."

I was feeling more anxious with each word. Ricky was beside me. I looked around before reaching for his hand. He pulled away, and I brought my hand back down. That hurt. More than anything this preacher could say. And he wasn't finished either.

"What is the best way to deal with young people in our families or congregation who might come out as gay?" he asked. "There are many options that I've heard proposed. Some have suggested to love them and accept them for who they are. No, that's not the right way to deal with the problem."

He took a sip of water and then raised his voice even more. "We need to lead them back to God, and sometimes that involves us being firm with them. I like to call that tough love."

I cringed. My parents used the term *tough love* when they administered corporal punishment. It was weird to hear this pastor use the same term.

The pastor continued with an anecdote. "There was once a family in our congregation who found out that their teenage son was gay and had a secret boyfriend. Do you know what they did?" The silence was so thick, I could feel it. "They took him to a church that had a program to help young people like this."

I got lost in my thoughts again. Was that something that my parents would do to me? Send me to some program like that?

"Contrary to what you might hear in the media, this is not some cruel conversion therapy program. No, it is a loving and compassionate counseling retreat where they meet with youth pastors who guide them through these emotions and help them understand God's purpose for their life." These last words were met by thunderous applause from the entire crowd. It was deafening, and it forced me to hold my hands over my ears in an attempt to block out the noise.

Once everyone calmed down, he continued one final time. "And let me leave you with this Bible passage. *Know ye not that the unrighteous shall not inherit the kingdom of God? Be not deceived: neither fornicators, nor idolaters, nor adulterers, nor effeminate, nor abusers of themselves with mankind, nor thieves, nor covetous, nor drunkards, nor revilers, nor extortioners, shall inherit the kingdom of God.*"

Everyone was dead silent, myself included. He had everyone's attention.

"What does this passage mean when it refers to 'abusers of themselves with mankind'? That is referring to the modern-day homosexual, and according to these verses, someone who is living that lifestyle can never enter Heaven."

As we filed out into the open air later that afternoon, I hardly paid any attention to anyone else. There were so many things going through my head. *If my parents found out, would they send me to a conversion therapy camp too?*

I continued to think about this the entire way home. Ricky sat beside me, but we didn't exchange any words either. There was still tension between us. That made this even worse. I was experiencing mixed emotions, and I wished I didn't have to go through that alone. I laid my head against the window and tried to fall asleep.

When I opened my eyes again, something seemed strange. I wasn't on the bus. I wasn't at home. *Where was I?*

I looked around, and everything was black. I couldn't see more than six inches in front of my face. Off in the distance, I saw something. A flicker, maybe. When I saw it again, I made my way there to see what it was.

I took a few steps, but as I got closer, I got a strange feeling. It started in the pit of my stomach and soon filled my entire chest cavity. With every step I took, my feet got heavier and heavier, as if they were turning into lead.

After a dozen steps, I stopped. It was getting too difficult. I bent over to catch my breath and sweat trickled down my face and dripped to the ground. Then I noticed something. As my sweat dripped, it turned into vapor as it hit the floor. It was still dark, but I could hear the sizzle, and I caught the faint glimpse of the steam with each drop that fell. I was confused at first, but then it occurred to me that my sweat wasn't just from exerting myself. It was getting warm. Warmer than when I first found myself there.

I looked up and my destination was just ahead. Ten feet more and I could reach it. My curiosity got the best of me, and I took another step forward.

I heard something, and I strained my ears to hear better. It sounded far away, off in the distance somewhere. It was muffled. *Was it coming from the other side of that door, perhaps?*

I waited to see if I could hear it again, and sure enough, there it was. It was definitely screams. *But from who?* I was alone. The more I listened, the more baffled I became. I couldn't make sense of it. I took another step forward. And another one. I stopped again. It was too much effort.

As I rested, my eye caught something else. There was a bright light coming from up above. I shielded my eyes, as it was too strong. I couldn't see anything, but I could sense another presence. Someone else was there.

"Jeremiah," a voice said to me.

"Yes?" I replied.

"Do you know why you are here?" the voice replied.

"No," I replied. "Who are you?"

"You are here to make an important decision," it said, ignoring my question.

"What decision?" I asked, feeling more and more apprehensive.

"A decision that will impact your eternal salvation," the voice continued. "I think you know what I mean."

I hesitated to answer. I knew what he meant. I asked, "Is it, is it a sin to be gay?"

I didn't get a reply, and I tried again. "That over there, is that hell?" I pointed towards the door I tried to reach mere moments ago.

"Only you can decide where you will spend eternity," the voice said. I was annoyed. I wanted him, or her, to just answer me straight and tell me what was going on.

"I get that," I said. "But what decision is the correct one? How can I know?"

"You will know in your heart," it said back to me. "Think about what you have read in my Word?"

"Your Word?" I repeated. "The Bible? Are you God?"

Again, silence.

"Please, I need you to tell me the truth," I begged. "Is it a sin to be gay or not? Will it send me to hell?"

Still no reply. I felt as if I knew the answer already. I didn't need to hear it said out loud. As I grappled with these thoughts, the light dimmed as it went away.

"Wait!" I yelled at it. "Stop! Don't go yet, please! I have more questions!" And then everything went black.

I jumped up. I wasn't yet sure where I was, but someone was with me. "It's okay. It was just a dream." That voice. I recognized it.

I opened my eyes. I realized we were still driving down the highway. I looked over and Ricky was beside me. His face was filled with concern.

"Are you okay?" he asked me.

"Yea," I mumbled. "I'm fine. Where are we?"

"We're almost home," he replied. He put his hand on my lap, but I abruptly pushed it away.

"What's the matter?" he asked. "It's dark. No one can see us."

But that's not what was bothering me. It was something else. I knew by the look on his face that I was hurting him again. But I had to think through things first. I put my head in my hands. I never felt as conflicted as I did at that moment.

CHAPTER 6

The next morning, I woke up with a massive headache. I couldn't even turn on the light because my head hurt so badly. My mom let me stay home from school. I lay in bed most of the day but couldn't sleep as the new baby cried for the better part of the day.

There were so many things that I had to think about while I lay there in bed. *Were Ricky and I okay?* Things had been tense between us the day before. I still wasn't sure what his problem was. He was getting more and more daring in public, but after his friends saw us at the arcade, we had to be more careful. I couldn't risk having anyone else catch us.

I didn't mean to be rude to him, but he was being overly pushy. It terrified me that someone would see, and the news would make its way to my parents.

Besides that, I was having doubts about whether I should even pursue this relationship. What that speaker said at the conference got to me. *Was I really going to go to hell for being gay?* I tried, but couldn't get that idea out of my head. It echoed everything that I'd been told my entire life.

I sat up and wrapped my arms around my knees. The curtains were drawn over my window and so my room was dark, despite it being almost 2:00 PM. I looked around. I needed to clean my room, since I had just dumped everything on the floor after returning home. I'd get to it later. I wasn't in the mood now.

I sighed and tossed my covers aside. I heard my baby sister outside crying at the top of her lungs. I ignored it as best as I could and picked up a lined journal that lay on my bedside table. I turned on my lamp and opened the book to the first blank page that I could find.

I found a black pen and sat there for a few moments, unsure of where to start. Finally, I put pen to paper and jotted down the following message:

Dear Ricky, I want to apologize for how I was on our trip. I didn't mean to be rude or hurt you. I know you just wanted affection and I'm sorry I kept saying no. I was so scared of somebody seeing us, but I shouldn't have reacted the way I did. I understand if you hate me, but I think maybe we need to take a break from each other. I'm not suggesting breaking up, but I need some time and space to think clearly about things first before we take our relationship any further. I hope you understand. Please forgive me.

Love Always,

Jeremiah

I sighed as I ripped the page out and shut the journal. *What was I getting myself into?* I got out of bed and took a hot shower.

My headache was gone by dinner time, and I went to school the following day. The school week went by as normal. I made sure not to cause any problems. I did my work, kept to myself, and waited for Friday to arrive.

For Friday's youth night, we met at the church for our Bible Study, and then went down to the local bowling alley where we ordered pizza and bowled for a couple of hours. My chest still felt heavy, and I wasn't in the mood, but my parents wouldn't let me stay home. I also had to talk to Ricky eventually, so I might as well get it over with as soon as possible.

As usual, I was the first one there, but Ricky arrived soon afterwards. We had about fifteen minutes until we started, so we had time to talk. I made eye contact with him, and I felt nauseous right away. This was going to be awkward, I knew it, but I smiled at him all the same and he returned my smile. His face looked natural, unlike how I felt.

"Hey," I said to him. "Is it okay if we go for a walk?" I could feel the note I wrote to him in my jacket pocket.

"Yea, sure," he replied, and we headed upstairs. We found a quiet corner that was hidden from the main entrance.

"I miss you," he said to me before I could say anything, and he took both of my hands in his. He looked at me, smiled, then kissed me. I was taken back.

"I missed you too," I stammered. "But before you say or do anything, I want to apologize."

"Apologize for what?" he asked. "Oh, for at the church? Forget about it. I was excited to be with you for the whole weekend and wasn't being careful. I should have listened when you told me to stop."

I didn't expect this at all. "I'm sorry," I said, almost sobbing, and I wrapped my arms tight around his neck. "I'm so sorry."

When we broke apart, I held his cheeks in my hands and looked him straight in the eyes. "I'm so sorry. I love you so much."

"I love you too," he replied, and we kissed again, but then stopped abruptly as we heard footsteps.

"I guess we better go back," I said. We walked past the foyer and joined more kids who were making their way downstairs. I reached into my jacket and crumpled up the note I intended to give him.

We had a wonderful evening. After our Bible study, we walked as a group down to the local bowling alley and spent the evening there.

It was Ricky's first time, and I showed him how to hold the ball and throw it properly. We were on the same team. We ended up losing our first game, but won the next one as we practiced and gradually improved.

I was sad when it was time to go home, but I'd see Ricky again on Sunday, and that kept me going. In the van on the way home, a thought occurred to me. Ricky and I had this great bond. *How could I go to hell for that? Go to hell for what? Loving somebody? Isn't that what the Bible was all about in the first place? About loving others?*

As soon as I got home, I ran into my room and reached for my Bible. I came across a verse not too long ago and bookmarked it. It was in Matthew and read: *Jesus said unto him, 'Thou shalt love the Lord thy God with all thy heart, and with all thy soul, and with all thy mind. This is the first and great commandment. And the second is like unto it, thou shalt love thy neighbour as thyself. On these two commandments hang all the law and the prophets.'*

I looked up and realized I could now think clearly. These were Jesus' own words I was reading. I wouldn't go to hell for following his most important commandment, right?

I felt all of my anxieties and stress lift in that moment, and when I went to bed, I had the most peaceful sleep I could remember.

June went by fast. At the end of the month, a group of Japanese high school students would visit our town for a week. I hadn't been studying Japanese recently as I had so many other things going on, but I was going to get back at it again.

I contacted the town office and told them I was studying Japanese and I asked if I could get involved somehow and meet the students. To my surprise, my school arranged for the students to come and have a tour of our school. I rolled my eyes as I knew the school was going to take it as an opportunity to evangelize them.

They would also see the public school, the judo hall, and have a farewell party at the community center. The town said that it would be okay for me to come out and meet them. I was excited for this and now set aside an hour every day to plug away at my Japanese studies.

On top of all this, Ricky's mom asked me to go to the Philippines with them in August, before school resumed again. I assumed my parents would say no, but much to my surprise, they let me. My mom and Mrs. Vergara were becoming close friends and my mom trusted her. My parents were discussing when they could take me into the city to apply for a passport. It would be my first time leaving the country and I couldn't ask for a better person to go with. Ricky and I going overseas together. Electricity ran through my body as I thought about it.

It was the last day of school when the Japanese exchange students visited our school. We had just finished lunch and were putting away our desks, which would go into storage until the end of

August.

The delegation consisted of five students and two adult chaperones. A couple of people from our town office were with them, too.

The students were all about the same age as me. They seemed shy as they looked around the room. Mr. Johnson introduced himself and the rest of the school staff, and then invited them to stand up at the front to address us.

One of the Japanese chaperones, a woman who was about forty years old, came forward and spoke in English. She only had a slight accent.

"Good morning, everyone," she said. "My name is Ms. Watanabe, and I have come with the students to have a tour of your beautiful town. Thank you very much for welcoming us. It is very much appreciated."

Everyone was quiet as we listened. "The others don't speak English, but let me introduce them to you. This is Taro, Mari, Ayako, Yumi, and Kenji, and this is their math teacher, Mr. Suzuki."

A round of polite applause followed, and Mr. Johnson stepped forward. "Thank you very much for coming to visit our town. We are happy that you're enjoying your stay. We will head upstairs where you will have a chance to tell us more about yourselves, and allow our students to ask some questions."

Upstairs, they stood at the pulpit while we took a seat in the pews to listen to them. Through their interpreter and the use of images displayed on a projector, they explained about their town, which was the same size as ours. It was a small rural community, surrounded by farmer's fields. It was my dream to go to Japan. Maybe I would even work and live there, but when I thought of Japan, I pictured Tokyo with its flashing neon lights, trendy shopping districts, and crowded yet futuristic train system.

Looking at the images displayed by the projector, I saw a whole other side of Japan I'd never imagined before. A small town that looked just as quiet and simple as my own. According to them, to get to Tokyo from their town, they had to drive almost an hour to a small airport which had four flights a day to and from Tokyo and that was it. The flight itself was ninety minutes.

It surprised me, but I listened intently to every word. The students spoke in Japanese and Ms. Watanabe interpreted for them. I realized my Japanese wasn't as good as I thought it was. They spoke so fast, and I could barely understand a word they said.

I tried not to let that bother me too much, and I focused on the students themselves. I thought Taro was cool. He looked to be about sixteen and he had his hair styled in a way our school would never approve of. He also had a single earring in his left ear and wore a silver chain around his neck. I thought he was cute. I shook my head. *What was I thinking?* I already had a boyfriend.

There were three girls. Mari was pretty, with long hair and thick-rimmed glasses. Ayako was a little overweight and had a couple of pimples on her cheek. She smiled the entire time and seemed more outgoing and friendly than the others. Yumi was short, but had a pleasant smile, albeit she looked to be the shyest of all of them.

Then there was the other boy, Kenji. He was also short, about the same as Yumi, but had a muscular physique and I could tell that he did some kind of sport. *Judo perhaps?* My eyes went back to Taro though. He was the one I wanted to meet and talk with the most. I'd try to get a chance.

After their presentation was over, they opened up the floor to questions. This was my chance to show off my Japanese skills. They answered three questions before I had the courage to raise my hand. They took another question, and then Mr. Johnson pointed to me.

I cleared my throat and hesitated a second, and then I spoke. It was the first time I ever spoke in Japanese to native speakers. "What do you think of our town?" I asked. There was silence for a moment and I waited for a response. I only waited about five seconds, but many thoughts rushed through my mind in that short time.

Was my pronunciation okay? I asked myself. *Oh, I think I mixed up the word for town and city.*

It was Ms. Watanabe who replied to me. She said, in English, "Oh, you can speak Japanese? You speak it very well."

I looked down at my shoes. My face was probably beet red. Ms. Watanabe turned to the kids and said something. Then Mari replied to me, slowly and in Japanese. "We like it very much. It's a nice town."

Ms. Watanabe translated for everyone else, but I wasn't paying attention. I was too preoccupied. *I understood that. I really understood what she said.*

Once the questions finished, Mr. Johnson gave them a quick overview of our school and what our beliefs were. I was tense when I heard this. It felt preachy, like they were doing some evangelizing while our guests were here. It seemed rude, but this was what my school was like, after all.

I was able to talk with the students for a few minutes before they left, and was pleasantly surprised to find my Japanese was better than I thought. The next day would be the farewell dinner for them organized by the town, so I'd be able to see them again before they left.

That night after dinner, I sat down at my desk and pulled out my Japanese study book. I spent thirty minutes studying vocabulary that I might need for the next day.

I was excited that after all the time I dedicated to studying, I could communicate in Japanese. It was an exhilarating feeling.

As I read my book and thought back to the day's events, something occurred to me. I was really attracted to Taro. Was it because he was so cool looking? Or was I developing a crush on him?

I shook my head at the silly notion. Of course, I wasn't. I had a boyfriend, and I was loyal. I would never think like that about another boy. *Or would I?*

That night, while I was sound asleep, I was transported to another place. I opened my eyes and looked around. I was in a classroom. Not my classroom. It was a real classroom, in a public school. A real school.

I looked down, and I had a desk in front of me. Not like the cubicle I was used to. I had a couple of books on my desk, and I picked them up, looking them over. They were written in Japanese. I couldn't read them. The kanji characters were too advanced for me.

I looked around at my surroundings. The classroom was large and there was a nice breeze from an open window. The next thing I noticed was that everybody was wearing a school uniform, but it differed from what we wore in my school.

I looked down at my own clothes. I was dressed in the same uniform as the other boys. I had on black leather shoes, gray pants, a white dress shirt, and a black blazer on top. I thought it looked quite smart.

I turned to my right to look at the boy sitting beside me, and I jumped back in surprise. I recognized my neighbor right away. It was Taro.

His hair was tamer than when I first met him, and he was wearing an identical uniform to mine. Other than that, he looked the same. I gave him a smile, but he didn't notice. He was too busy taking notes. That's when I noticed the notebook sitting in front of me. I glanced up at the whiteboard and saw a list of mathematical formulas that we must have been expected to write. I picked up a pencil and began to write.

I didn't recognize many of the symbols in the formula. My private school was so focused on religious teachings that they must have forgotten to teach us things that we might actually need to know.

After about five minutes of jotting down the math formulas which I didn't really understand, I noticed something else out of the corner of my eye. I looked up and glanced to my right and Taro was still there. It occurred to me I was developing a crush on him. He was just so cool. Nothing against Ricky, of course. Ricky was nice and sweet, and we got along great. But Taro had something different. I couldn't quite put my finger on it, but I started liking him more and more.

I turned my head to the left and my jaw fell open at what I saw. There was Ricky, sitting beside me, writing away. He was also dressed in the same school uniform. This was just too weird. I couldn't make sense of it.

Here I was, sitting in between these two boys. My boyfriend

and another boy I also found quite attractive. Was someone trying to tell me something? I tried to push these thoughts out of my head, and I bent over to continue writing. But I couldn't concentrate. I looked back at Taro. *If I had the chance to choose him over Ricky, would I?*

As these thoughts ran through my head, everything went pitch black. I dropped my pencil and looked around. I couldn't see farther than a foot in front of me.

I looked around, feeling very confused. I jumped at the sound of a loud bang. There was a spotlight that lit up a nearby chair. It was Ricky. He was sitting there, not saying anything. His eyes were vacant, and he wasn't showing any emotion. He just stared straight ahead. He was still wearing his school uniform.

Another bang and another spotlight. This time, on my other side. I didn't have to guess who I would see. It was Taro. Same thing. Quiet. No emotion. Still in his school uniform.

What was the meaning of this? Was I supposed to choose between them? I looked over at Ricky. We had so many good times together, and he was so sweet to me. His family treated me as one of their own.

Then I looked over at Taro. I hardly even knew him. I met him once, spoke to him only briefly. But I couldn't get over how cool he seemed. His style, his demeanor, his voice. Everything.

I put my head in my hands. I couldn't be forced to choose. I was with Ricky and that was final. I wasn't a cheater. *Or was I?* I looked back up at Taro. I hesitated and then looked back down. I couldn't be forced to choose. I just couldn't.

When I looked back up, everything was black again and I couldn't see a thing.

BEEP BEEP BEEP

That was my alarm clock that sat beside my bed. I groped around in the dark but couldn't find it.

BEEP BEEP BEEP

The sound continued. I reached around more, and my hand touched something hard and plastic. Found it!

I opened my eyes, and I was sitting in my bedroom again, the alarm clock in my hand. I turned my alarm off, and something dawned on me. It was Saturday. *Why did I set my alarm?*

I groaned and laid back down, closing my eyes again.

That evening, my mom drove me to town where the farewell dinner for our Japanese guests would be held. Ricky was going to join as well, and I bumped into him at the entrance.

"Hey," I said to him. "You look nice."

"Thanks," he said with a smile. He was wearing navy dress pants, a white dress shirt, and a navy blazer. It was strikingly similar to the school uniforms that we all wore in my dream.

I was also dressed up. I had on black dress pants and a plaid shirt. It wasn't to my liking, but all of my good clothes were in the wash.

When we were inside the community hall, I recognized Eddy, one of the kids from Ricky's party. We made our way over to him.

He looked up at us and smiled. "Hi guys," he said.

"Oh, I forgot you met Eddy before," Ricky said to me. "His family hosted one of the students."

"Oh, really?" I said, surprised. "Who stayed at your house?"

"Him," he said, and pointed over at the other end of the table. I looked over and saw that he was pointing at Taro. He was talking with Ms. Watanabe and the rest of the delegation.

"Yes, I met them," I said. "They visited my school yesterday."

"Mind if we sit here with you guys?" Ricky asked.

"Yea, sure," he said, and he scooted over to make room for us.

When it was time to eat, Taro came over and joined us. He recognized me and greeted me warmly. My stomach felt like it was being tied in knots.

Remembering the Japanese I practiced the previous night, I said to him, "This is my friend, Ricky. He's learning Japanese too."

He had a look of surprise on his face. "Really?" he said. "That's great."

I loved this language skill proved useful. I felt a little guilty knowing the thoughts I had about Taro while Ricky was sitting beside me. *It's not like he's gay,* I told myself. *Nothing will happen, so don't worry about it.*

We had a wonderful evening. Communicating with Taro in Japanese wasn't as difficult as I anticipated, even though I didn't understand everything. Taro brought with him this cool little electronic device. It was a portable dictionary. I'd never seen anything like it before. Much more convenient than the thick paperback dictionary that I had at home, so it helped us when we hit a communication barrier.

A couple of the girls came over and joined us. Before I knew it, Ricky and I both had their email addresses and they made us promise to go visit them in Japan someday and we both agreed that we would. They lived in Hokkaido, and on the map that they showed me I saw it was quite far from Tokyo, but I was excited at the prospect of traveling there.

I never left the country before, but I would go to the Philippines with Ricky and his family in August. I suggested making a side trip to Japan, but as Filipino passport holders, Ricky and his family would all need to apply for tourist visas, and they decided it would be too complicated and take too much time.

I decided I'd save up and try to go alone as soon as I could. Or maybe with Ricky, if he could accompany me.

I was supposed to visit my relatives in the Netherlands as well, but that was going to have to wait. I would go to Japan first.

The night ended with the student delegation standing up in front of everyone and, with the help of their interpreter, Ms. Watanabe, they gave a short speech about what they thought of the United States, and of our small town.

It was sad to say goodbye, but I had their contact information and would definitely go to visit them in Japan someday. Maybe even the following year, if my parents allowed it. I had been trying for a year to convince them to let me go to Japan as an exchange student, and they refused. Maybe they would be okay with me going for a short summer exchange trip instead?

Mrs. Vergara offered to drive me home, so my parents didn't have to wait around in town all evening. During the drive, Ricky and I talked about our upcoming trip to the Philippines.

It was just over a month away. The next week, my dad was going to take me into the city to apply for my passport and I still couldn't believe that they were allowing me to go. They had never afforded me such freedom before.

Ricky's family lived in a rural area, seven hours from Manila, and we were going to spend two weeks there. Ricky said they lived near the beach. I had never been to the sea before, and all the new prospects this trip offered excited me.

Mrs. Vergara drove, so Ricky leaned in, and whispered in my ear, "I have my own room in our family's house. We'll have lots of time alone during our trip," and he gave me a wink, followed by a kiss on the cheek. What he said made me feel aroused. It looked like there would be even more to look forward to than I thought.

I reached around in the dark and found his hand. I gave it a squeeze and held it for the duration of the drive home.

I was exhausted by the time I climbed into bed. Exhausted, but my mind was wide awake at the same time. I had a busy and exciting day, and there were so many things to think about.

Meeting the Japanese students, my upcoming trip to the Philippines with Ricky, my planned trip to Japan.

And with these thoughts going through my head, I fell asleep.

CHAPTER 7

I pulled out my passport and looked at it for what seemed like the millionth time. I couldn't believe that this was finally happening. I looked at Ricky, who was walking beside me, and we exchanged smiles.

We just touched down at the Los Angeles International Airport. It was a few minutes after 4:00 PM and we had lots of time to kill. Our flight with Philippine Airlines, PR103, would depart for Manila shortly before midnight.

Our flight from Chicago took about four hours. It was my first time on an airplane, and I was nervous when we first took off, but I found I enjoyed the flight. That was a good thing because I had a fifteen hour flight coming up.

I was traveling with Ricky, his parents, and older sisters, Angel and Jessa. It was their first time going back since moving to the United States, and everyone was excited. Especially me, this being my first trip overseas.

It took ten minutes to walk from Terminal 4 to Terminal B, where the international departures were located. I always loved learning about foreign countries and cultures, and I looked in awe at the different signs above the departure gates. I saw a flight to Dubai that was about to board. Another one for Beijing and Paris. I saw another gate that would soon board a flight to Istanbul.

It was like the entire world was all here in one place, and I looked around in amazement.

"It's a lot to take in, isn't it?" Mrs. Vergara said to me.

"Yes," was all I said as I continued looking around.

Our gate number hadn't been announced yet, so we found a quiet area to sit, and put our stuff down. All I had with me was a backpack. I had a sweater inside, as well as a couple of books, some toiletries, and snack food. My clothes were in my duffel bag that was with the checked luggage.

I sat down and dropped my backpack on the floor. Ricky took a seat beside me. There were so many people from many different countries. It was a lot to take in.

"Are you guys hungry?" Mr. Vergara asked us.

"Starving!" Ricky said.

"Here," he said, and he gave us a fifty-dollar bill. "Go get yourselves some food. I'm sure you don't want to hang around us old people the entire time."

"Thank you," I said, and I followed Ricky. We looked for signs as we tried to find a place to eat.

"Your parents are so cool," I said. "Mine would never let me go off on my own."

"Yea, they're alright," he said, absentmindedly. "What do you want to eat?"

I looked around. There was what looked like a food court with various fast food joints. Off to the side, there were some sit-down restaurants, too.

Ricky looked at me mischievously. "So, can we make this a date?"

I laughed. He was so cute sometimes. But he had a point. We were finally out on our own without any adult supervision. I still couldn't bring myself to kiss him in public, though.

"Let's try this," he said as he pulled me by my hand. We stood in front of a western-style restaurant that had a bar and lounge off to the side. It had private booths in the corner, so we went in and took a seat. We both ordered a burger and fries.

"Are you excited?" he asked me as we waited for our food. I couldn't help looking into his brown eyes as I sat there.

"Yea," I said. "But the flight is so long."

"Don't worry about it," he said. "We can just watch a movie and then sleep. It won't be that bad."

"I hope not," I said.

"Come here," he said to me.

"What?" I wasn't sure what he meant. He stood up and leaned

into me.

"Come here," he repeated. "I want to tell you something."

I was a little confused, but I stood up and leaned into him. He gave me a quick kiss on the mouth and then sat back down as he burst into laughter.

I hid my face as I sat down. It was probably bright red. I was so embarrassed.

"I said not to do that in public," I said.

"What's the matter?" he said. "Look around. No one cares. This is liberal Los Angeles after all."

"I guess," I said as I glanced around the restaurant. No one was even looking in our direction. "But still, don't do that. Please. It makes me nervous."

"Okay," he said. "Suit yourself."

I felt bad. I hoped I wasn't annoying him, but I was so self-conscious about it. Could you imagine if his parents saw? And then they told my parents? I would probably die.

We spent about two hours in the restaurant. There was a football game on the TV, so it was rowdy near the bar area, but it was quiet and private where we sat. It was almost 6:00 PM when we decided we had better get back to the rest of the group before they worried about us.

As we made our way back to where they were waiting, I looked at the signs above the different departure gates again. There was a flight that was about to board heading to Seoul, another one bound for Sao Paulo, and another one was going to Hong Kong.

Then I stopped. Ricky noticed and turned back to look at me. "What's the matter?" he asked.

"Look," I pointed at one sign. The flight had already departed, but the destination was still displayed. *Tokyo.*

"You have no idea how badly I want to be on that flight," I said.

"You don't want to go with me?" Ricky asked.

I let out a chuckle. "I meant with you, of course," I said. "Next year, I'm definitely making it happen. And you're coming with me."

"Come on," he said with a laugh, and we found the rest of his family. We still had over five hours until our flight. I wanted to pull out a book I borrowed from the library for this trip. It was an epic fantasy about a girl who fell into a well and ended up in an ancient world filled with demons and sorcerers. My parents would never approve, so I hid it away with my things when I packed. Ricky's family was much more chill about TV programs and books. I would enjoy so much more freedom during these two weeks.

I was too tired and anxious for the trip, so I forewent the book and tried to rest. Ricky sat beside me, but he didn't seem tired at all. He was talking animatedly with his family. The last thing I remember was him asking me if I wanted a chocolate bar. He was going to run to the vending machine. With sleep in my eyes, I shook my head.

The next thing I knew, someone was shaking me awake. "What's going on?" I asked as I checked my watch. It was 10:50 PM.

"Come on," Ricky said, as he gave me another shake. "We're going to board soon."

There was something being called on over the PA system. "That's our flight," Ricky said. "Let's go."

I slung my backpack over my shoulder and went with him. His parents and sisters were just ahead, looking for the gate. A crowd of people already formed a line. Mrs.Vergara was double checking the seat numbers on our boarding passes and I pulled out my passport from my back pocket. I was excited that I could finally use it.

Twenty minutes later, our boarding group was called. I showed my passport to the attendant; she scanned my boarding pass, and then we walked down the bridge towards the aircraft.

My insides felt all tight and scrunched together. I wanted to squeeze Ricky's hand, but everyone else was with us, and so I resisted the urge. I looked out one of the small windows. Everything outside was dark, but I could see the faint flashing lights of various other airplanes on the tarmac.

I tried to ignore the butterflies in my stomach. I gripped my passport tightly as I approached the flight attendants and showed them my boarding pass. They pointed us to our seats, and we headed down the aisle.

I took one last look at my boarding pass. My seat number was 53A and Ricky's was 53B. They were located behind the wing on the left side of the plane. I looked around the interior and was taken back by how massive it was inside.

I didn't know much about airplanes, but after studying the pamphlet in the back seat pocket, I found out that we were flying in a Boeing 777-300ER. The seats were arranged in a 3-4-3 configuration, so ten seats wide. Three by the window, four in the middle section, and then another three by the other window.

My seat was against the window, with Ricky right beside me. Angel was on his other side. Jessa sat in the row ahead of us with their parents. I pushed my backpack under the seat in front of me and turned to look at Ricky. He was all smiles.

"You okay?" he asked me.

"I'm fine," I replied. "Why? Do I look worried?"

He laughed and shook his head. He squeezed my hand quickly before fastening his seatbelt. I followed suit.

We pulled away from the gate fifteen minutes later and taxied out onto the runway. This was my second time taking off, and it was by far the most exhilarating thing I had experienced in my life. That included the time that Ricky coaxed me to go down the *Drop of Doom* at the water park.

No, this felt different. It was exciting. At first, I tensed up, but then I felt weightless and relaxed. I looked at Ricky. His head was laid back, and he seemed quite relaxed too. Much more than I was. He looked so content, I thought he would fall asleep.

The flight went well, helped in part by who my travel partner was. This was the first of many trips that I would make in my life.

The travel books I read always talked about how bad airplane food was, but I didn't find it to be half bad. We had a type of rice curry, a side salad, a bun with a slice of cheese and butter, and a small serving of mango ice cream for dessert. Ricky and I both had a can of coke with our meal.

After we finished eating, I made a quick trip to the bathroom and then settled in for the rest of our long flight.

I flipped through the movies on the in-flight entertainment

system. There was an assortment of both Hollywood and foreign films. I spent some time scrolling, and then settled on a film I had seen advertised, but I knew my parents wouldn't let me go see it in the cinema. This was my chance, and I turned the movie on.

I was happy to have this alone time with Ricky, but given the location of our seats, we couldn't hear each other well over the constant hum of the engine, so we were left to our own devices.

I watched two movies and then I found the music collection. I put on some soothing pop music and went to sleep. When I woke up, everything was still dark. I wasn't sure how long I slept for.

I checked my watch. It was 1:00. Was that night or afternoon? I wasn't sure, but it still looked like nighttime outside. I looked over at Ricky and saw that he was sound asleep. I had the urge to go to the bathroom again, but Angel was watching a movie and I didn't want to interrupt her.

I went back to the entertainment system and realized that it had a time display. It indicated that the time in Los Angeles was 1:00 PM, while at our destination in Manila, it was 4:00 AM. We were scheduled to arrive in an hour and a half.

I changed the time on my watch. After that, I looked at the interactive map on my screen, and it showed we were approaching the Philippine Islands. We were almost there. I shivered with excitement.

It wasn't long before the cabin lights turned back on and Ricky woke up. The flight attendants brought us our pre-arrival meal, which consisted of a cup of yogurt, a small bowl of fruit, and orange juice. I was starving. The food wasn't enough to fill me up, but it was something.

Finally, we touched down at Manila's Ninoy Aquino International Airport. By the time we cleared customs, immigration, and collected our luggage, it was almost 7:00 AM. Despite having slept for half the flight, I yawned loudly. Mrs. Vergara chuckled.

"Feeling sleepy?" she said to me. I nodded. Ricky, who was standing beside me, wore a blank expression. He looked as tired as I felt.

So, this was the Philippines? The first thing that I noticed was how sticky I felt. The air smelt a little like the sauna at a swimming pool. This was what humidity was like.

As we stepped outside, I saw that the sun was already coming out. It was quite warm already, but I knew it would get even warmer.

Mr. Vergara had an eight-person van already ordered for the six of us. We loaded our luggage in and took off into the congested streets of Manila.

I looked out the window with wide eyes. My mind was too stimulated to feel tired anymore. This was a whole new world to me. Everything seemed so chaotic. Cars and motorcycles were pushing their way through the crowded streets along with these really colorful weird looking vehicles that Ricky told me were called jeepneys. I wanted to ride in one when I got the chance.

Another thing that struck me was how packed everything was. I didn't see any empty space at all. It was all taken over by buildings that were tightly crammed together.

It took us forty minutes to get to the bus station in Quezon City, and then we took a seven hour bus ride north. Our destination was a small village in the rural province of La Union.

The view of the countryside was a welcome change from the congested and dirty city, but fatigue got the better of me, so Ricky and I slept for most of the trip. We got out at a pit stop to use the restroom as well as grab a drink and some snacks. We quickly consumed them and went back to sleep.

We woke up again as we entered the city of San Fernando. I checked my watch. It was 3:00 PM. This had been a long day, and I was exhausted by the time we climbed out of the bus.

San Fernando, at first glance, looked similar to Manila, but smaller and not as crowded. The bus station was in front of a small strip mall. While Mr. Vergara and the bus attendant unloaded the luggage, Ricky and I took off to find the restroom.

"So, what do you think?" he asked me as we were walking along the side of the building.

"It's cool," I said. I wasn't sure how to explain it yet. I needed more time to take things in.

"Over here," Ricky said and pointed to a sign that read *Toilet*. The one we used at the previous stop took some getting used to. It was literally just a hole in the floor. I was pleased that this one was more western style, with proper toilets and a row of urinals along the wall.

We finished our business and then we looked around. We were all alone. Ricky gave me a smirk. I acknowledged and gave my consent with a nod. I walked up to him, and our lips met. We had been waiting so long to have this time alone.

We were at it for at least a full two minutes. I was exhausted and jet-lagged, but that moment gave me an infusion of energy.

We broke apart when we heard footsteps approaching outside. I glanced down and wiped my mouth, as if that was going to hide any evidence of anything.

The door opened, and we saw it was Mr. Vergara. "Hey, you boys finished?" he asked as he made his way to a urinal.

"Yep," Ricky said. "Meet you at the bus station." And we headed back to where everyone else was waiting.

We still had to be careful. I had so much more freedom with Ricky's family than I did back home, but when it came down to our relationship, that was still something we had to keep a secret. It hurt a little that we couldn't just be ourselves. I remember watching on the news about how Canada was legalizing same-sex marriage, and how in many places, including in the United States, there were big parades to celebrate gay people being able to live as they want.

I was so jealous that some people lived in a society where they could feel comfortable enough to live how they wanted. I didn't. I still enjoyed more freedom than I was accustomed to on this trip, but it still came with certain restrictions.

I got my wish to ride in a jeepney granted sooner than I expected. Ricky's Uncle Josef came to pick us up, and he owned his own jeepney.

Josef looked to be about forty. He was balding and had a bit of a stomach, but his demeanor was very jovial. His son, Markus, who was a little younger than Ricky—he looked to be about twelve—accompanied him.

The family began conversing rapidly in Tagalog. Earlier, Ricky's family tried to teach me some basic Tagalog words, but I forgot almost everything as I spent so much time studying Japanese. The only thing that came to mind at that moment was *Kamusta ka,* which I said when their attention turned to me. Everyone burst out laughing and I wished I'd stuck to English.

"Welcome to the Philippines," Uncle Josef said in heavily accented English, and he took my hand in his, gripping it firmly. "As the saying goes, it's more fun in the Philippines."

"Thank you," I said with a smile. "I'm happy to be here."

We loaded all of our luggage into the jeepney and took off. It amazed me just how colorful and artistically decorated it was. It was also awash in religious imagery. Bible verses on the side. A crucifix hanging from the front mirror. I read the Philippines was a deeply Catholic country, and now I could see for myself what that meant.

Riding in a jeepney was a unique experience. It was like a jeep with an elongated back end. There was a long bench on either side for people to sit on, and we kept our luggage in the middle. There was no door on the back, so we got a constant rush of wind and dust as we drove along the country road.

The drive took about an hour to get to their home. It was on the outskirts of a small village. We drove through the town, and some of the architecture reminded me of a Mexican-style pueblo I had seen in movies.

In the center was a town square overlooked by a large Catholic cathedral. It was the fanciest looking church I ever saw.

The house that we were staying at was on the top of a hill. It was made of brick and surrounded by a ten-foot wall topped with barbed wire.

All the other houses in the area were small single-room homes made of wood with tin roofs. The one Ricky's family lived in seemed like a mansion in comparison.

Ricky's grandma and grandpa met us when we arrived. They

didn't speak much English, but they were very outgoing and friendly. They sent out a couple of kids, presumably more of Ricky's cousins, to help carry the luggage in, as Grandma and a couple of aunts went right away to set the table. They already had a full meal waiting for us. My mouth watered.

"Ricky, show Jeremiah where you boys will sleep," Mrs. Vergara said. "Then you can go take a quick bath before we eat."

"Okay," Ricky said, and we went into the house. It was bigger than my home back in the States. I later learned that it had eight bedrooms and five bathrooms. It was massive and Ricky led me upstairs and to a simple room with a Queen bed and an air conditioner on the wall.

"It's nice," I said as I looked around. I dropped my suitcase in the corner, opened it, and took out a pair of clean underwear and a pair of shorts. I had been wearing a pair of jeans this entire time and I regretted it. My whole groin area felt like it would be rubbed raw.

"The shower is in the next room," Ricky said. "Do you want to go first? I can wait."

"You don't want to come in with me?" I asked with a mischievous smile.

"Not now," he said to me with a wink. "Too many people around. Someone will notice."

Fair point. I went and got cleaned up. I was disappointed when I saw that there was no hot water. I was hot and sticky, so the cool water felt good, but I didn't think I'd survive the whole two weeks without any warm water.

When I mentioned that to Ricky, he started laughing. "There is hot water," he said. "You have to turn the water heater on."

"The what?" I had no idea what that was.

"Come with me," he said, and he led me back to the bathroom, indicating a contraption on the wall. "You just turn this," he said, and he pointed to a dial. "Turn that and you get hot water."

"Oh," was all I could say. Well, that solved the problem.

It was about 5:00 PM when we ate and the food was so appetizing. There was lots of rice, various fried meats, grilled fish, slices of fresh mango, and my favorite, pork adobo.

The adults started drinking soon afterward. That took me by surprise, because back home my parents, and most of the families in our church, were very much against alcohol. One of our previous pastors was fired when it was discovered he enjoyed the occasional drink.

Ricky's family was also very religious and conservative, but here they were, drinking beer and having a good time. That was something I never saw in my church community back home.

It was getting dark, and someone set up a karaoke machine. Ricky said something to his mom, then he nudged me, and I followed him up the stairs.

In the bedroom, I took off my shorts, threw them in the corner, and fell on the bed in just my T-shirt and underwear. Rick did the same and lay down beside me.

"How do you feel?" he asked.

"It's just so much to take in," I said. "But I think it's going to be fun."

"It will be," Ricky said with a smile. He reached out, placed his hand on my stomach, and rubbed my stomach. "Feeling tired?" he asked.

I nodded. I got up, turned the light off, and rejoined him on the bed. He put his arm around me, and I turned to face him.

"I'm so happy to be here with you," I said. "I couldn't imagine coming here with anyone else." It was dark, but I could almost feel him smiling back at me.

He scooted a little closer, and we kissed. I wanted it to last for a long time, but I was exhausted from the trip and the events of the day. Soon I was sound asleep, without a care in the world. Ricky, my love, beside me.

I slept late the next day. Mrs. Vergara knocked on our door in the morning to tell us that breakfast was ready. She didn't come back again, and we went right back to sleep.

It was almost noon by the time I pulled myself out of bed. I took a shower and put on my shorts from the night before with a new T-shirt. I looked through my clothes. I only brought a couple of pairs of shorts. I packed mostly jeans. That wasn't smart, but it was too late now. I'd have to do laundry more often than anticipated. Either that or wear the same pair for longer than I probably should.

Ricky got up soon after, and we both headed downstairs together. There were so many people in the house, and I felt shy.

I didn't know how many lived in the house and how many had just come to visit, but it looked like all of his relatives were gathered together.

Ricky's parents and sisters weren't anywhere to be seen. We took a seat and readily helped ourselves to the food that was placed in front of us. We hardly said a word to each other as we dug in. I wasn't sure how to explain my feelings. I was hungry, but also tired. Not sleepy. I felt fatigued. This was what jet-lag felt like, I supposed.

Ricky's parents came back later. We were going to go to the beach that afternoon, so we ran upstairs and grabbed our trunks.

We spent the first few days around the family home, going to the nearby beach, and singing karaoke at night. We even went to San Fernando once to go to the shopping mall. Ricky and I got to spend time in the arcade and even went to the cinema. I was really enjoying myself and the newfound freedom I had.

    I dreaded having to go back home.

CHAPTER 8

I had been in the Philippines for a week already and was thoroughly enjoying myself. The first few days, I struggled with adapting to the time difference, and the humidity took some getting used to. Now I was acclimatized and with the program. We still had over a week left in our trip, and there were many things on the agenda.

I hadn't had as much time alone with Ricky as I hoped. Not during the day, anyway. We shared a room and bed at night, but usually by that time we were so tired that we just cuddled and went to sleep.

But on one sunny day, Mrs. Vergara allowed us to go off on our own. There was going to be a family wedding the next day, and tonight there was going to be a party to celebrate. The entire village would be there. But we had some free time beforehand.

We didn't go off completely on our own. Some of his cousins joined us as well. Three boys, all about the same age as us, or a little younger. Markus was one of them. The other two were Jon and Ronaldo. They were both friendly and outgoing.

We all headed down to a secluded corner of the beach and we spent a good part of the afternoon in the water. While Ricky and I wore swimming trunks, the other boys just went swimming in their underwear. That struck me as odd, but Ricky just told me that that was life in the countryside there.

As we enjoyed our time, Ricky kept getting close to me in the water and I kept reluctantly pushing him back.

"Not here," I hissed at him. "They'll see."

He laughed. "It's okay. They don't care."

"What? Really?"

Ricky laughed again. "My parents are the religious ones," he said. "The rest of the family goes to church, sure, but they're not so strict about it."

"Really?" I said. I wasn't sure if I was willing to test that hypothesis.

"Here," Ricky said. "Let me show you." With that, he called out to the other boys to get their attention. With them watching, he turned to me, grabbed my ass, and planted a long kiss right on my lips. I pulled back and my facial expression probably said it all. Ricky started laughing when our eyes met.

"It's okay," he told me. The other boys came over to us, and I could feel myself tense up.

"Are you guys boyfriends or something?" Ronaldo asked.

"Yep," Ricky said, and gave me another kiss.

"Cool," Jon said. "I kissed a boy once. It was fun."

"You guys are cool with this?" I asked with surprise.

They all laughed. "Yea, it's cool," Ronaldo said.

"What about your parents?" I asked. "Would they have a problem with it?"

"Maybe," Jon said. "But they're older. Different generation, you know?"

I nodded and smiled, then I threw my arms around Ricky and gave him a long, hard kiss. My first time to ever express my love openly. It felt exhilarating. This must have been what equal rights felt like. The ability to express our love the same way that any heterosexual couple could.

The rest of the afternoon went by fast, and we had a great time. We only climbed out of the water when it got dark. We didn't even put our clothes back on. We just dried off, picked up our stuff, and made our way back down the dusty dirt road.

His cousins weren't quite ready to go back to the house yet, and we took a detour. I waited with Ricky outside while his cousins went into a small shop.

"What are they buying?" I asked.

Ricky didn't reply, just gave a shrug. The boys exited the shop a couple of minutes later with a black plastic bag in their hands.

"What's that?" I asked.

"Come with us," Ronaldo said, and we went behind the shop and up a path that was partially obscured by the thick overgrowth of the trees. Their village sat on the edge of a vast jungle.

We walked for about five minutes until we came to a small clearing. The grass had been trampled flat. There were a few low stools to the side, and a garbage bag full of beer cans. It looked like this was a popular hang-out spot.

Ronaldo put the bag on the ground and pulled the stools over, placing them in a circle. "Here," he said. "Sit."

I took a seat, and he rummaged in the bag, pulling out a few cans of what looked like beer. He passed them around. I took one and held it, with no intention of doing anything. I still remembered what happened the last time I drank alcohol. It wasn't a pleasant experience.

The others, Ricky included, opened their cans and took a sip. Jon said something to Ricky in Tagalog, and they all turned to look at me.

"He asked if you drink beer or not," Ricky said.

I looked back at them awkwardly, not sure how to respond. I lied. "Sometimes."

"Okay," Ricky said. "Then drink." And they all took another drink. I cracked the can open, held it up to my lips, hesitated, and then took a small sip.

The boys were all chatting excitedly with one another. I couldn't understand what they were saying, so I sat in silence and pretended to listen. When they took a drink, I took a tiny sip as well.

I wasn't sure what to think. His cousins seemed really cool, and they were chill with us being gay, which I didn't expect. However, I didn't like drinking. I already had one bad experience with alcohol. At that time, we drank something much stronger than beer, but it still left a sour taste in my mouth for alcohol. Back home, the legal drinking age was twenty-one and here we were on the other side of the world, where that didn't seem to matter.

I checked my watch. It was getting late. We were going to have to get back soon for the party. Opposite of the customs back home, in the Philippines, they threw a big party, with music, dancing and alcohol, the night before the wedding. The actual ceremony was the morning after the party. We would all then go to the church for the formal service.

I sat there, lost in my thoughts, until the boys got my attention. "Hey, have you guys done it yet?" Ronaldo asked me.

"Did what?" I didn't know what he meant.

He snickered. "You know. Did you guys do the dirty?"

"Wha-? Oh, that?" I could feel myself blushing. Fortunately, it was too dark for them to notice. "No, not yet."

"Why not?" Jon asked.

I looked over at Ricky for support. I couldn't make out his facial expression in the dark, but he was sitting there drinking his beer and didn't seem to be paying attention to the conversation.

I looked back at the others and shrugged. "I don't know," I said. "Just haven't had the chance I guess."

"Well, you're out here, away from your family," Ronaldo said. "Why not do it here?"

"Here? In the jungle?" I couldn't believe what I was hearing.

They all burst out laughing. "No," Ronaldo said. "Not now. Just, while you're here on holiday."

"Oh," I said. "Yea, maybe."

"Here." He handed me something. It was a small orange piece of plastic. I held it up to the moonlight to see it better. It was a condom.

"It's for you guys," Jon said. "You should use it."

"Maybe," I said. "You guys, it's getting late. We should head back."

Ricky finally came back to the conversation. "Yea, sure," he said. "Let's go."

The music was already in full swing when we got back to the house. They had a large tent set up in an empty field across the road, and it seemed like the entire village had come out.

Ricky's three cousins were still in nothing but their underwear, and so they scurried off down to their homes to get dressed.

"Come on," Ricky said to me. "We should change too." We went upstairs, took a quick shower, and threw on a change of clothes. I wore a pair of jeans and a light gray T-shirt, while Ricky wore sweatpants and a black hoodie. He had this uncanny ability of looking so attractive while wearing something plain and casual.

Markus, Jon, and Ronaldo all joined in later, as well as many more cousins I hadn't met before. A temporary stage was set up at the one end of the tent, complete with a DJ and a full set of equipment. The music was pounding. I felt the ground vibrating evenly under my feet.

I noticed Mrs. Vergara dancing around the room with a couple of her relatives. She looked wasted. This was a glimpse into Ricky's family in a way I had never seen before, and it surprised me. I couldn't imagine what my parents would think if they knew.

"Come on," Ricky said to me, and he took me by the hand, leading me into the center of the dance floor. We started bobbing away to the beat. Jon and Ronaldo ran over to join us.

Ricky's sisters came over with a group of girls. *More cousins,* I presumed. They were all holding shot glasses in their hands and they downed the liquid, whatever it was.

"Are you having a good time?" Angel shouted to me over the sound of the music.

"Yea," I said.

"Come join us," Jessa said. "We're having our own party."

I looked at Ricky. He gave me a knowing look and nodded. We followed the girls to a nearby garage. Jon and Ronaldo came with us.

The garage was set up as a sort of storage shed, but on the one side was a small bedroom with a ratty mattress on the ground. I wasn't sure who slept there. It was my first time there.

The garage was dusty, with cobwebs covering every corner. Along the wall were a couple of old motorcycles hidden under a tarp. And a couple of karaoke machines sat against another wall collecting dust.

"Here," Jessa said to me. "Grab a chair." They set up a bunch of plastic chairs in a circle, and we all took a seat. Ronaldo pulled out a pack of cigarettes and started passing them around. Only a couple of people obliged, but that was enough. Soon the air was full of cigarette smoke. Angel and one of her cousins started pouring something into small glasses and they began passing them around.

"What is that?" I asked.

"Just a little pick-me-up," Jessa said as she passed me a glass. "It'll make the party better. I promise."

I looked at it. It had a slight reddish tinge. I brought it up to my nose and sniffed. It didn't smell all that bad. There was a slight trace of apple spice. Ricky turned to look at me and he held up his glass.

"Are you ready?" he asked.

"I guess so," I said, without much enthusiasm.

Everyone lifted their glasses and then downed them. I looked around the room. Everyone else seemed to do okay with it, and so I followed suit. The stuff tasted worse than it looked. I choked on it as soon as it went down. It was like my entire throat just seized up. Half of it ended up getting spit back out. What made its way down my throat burned.

No sooner had I recovered than someone took my glass, passed it back to Angel, and she refilled it. I tried to hold my hand up in protest, but another coughing fit took over. The glass, filled again, was placed back in my hand.

"You okay?" Angel asked me. "It's okay, just one more. Each one gets better."

She was barely done speaking and everyone except me downed their glasses. I stared at mine.

"Come on," Ricky whispered to me. "Hurry up. Just down it."

I sighed, held my breath, and brought the glass back to my lips. I took the smallest of sips. She was right. It was a little better. It didn't taste like poison this time. I tilted my head and downed the rest of the glass. I ended up choking and spitting it back out again. It tasted even worse than before. Everyone was laughing at me. When I finally recovered, I felt my face heat up.

"Here," one girl said, and she passed me a beer. "Just stick with this. It's easier."

"Thanks," I mumbled. I didn't like beer, but it was a welcome alternative to that other stuff. I happily opened the bottle and took a generous sip.

I looked at Ricky. His face was as red as I felt. I put my hand on his leg and he smiled back at me. We sat there and continued to drink for a while. I tried to ignore the smell of cigarettes as the smoke hung around in the air.

This turned out to be the place where the kids hung out and did things that their parents wouldn't approve of. Ricky's family seemed much cooler than mine, but they definitely wouldn't approve of these kids smoking and drinking. I set my beer bottle under my chair. If his parents came storming in, I'd rather that they didn't have anything to tell my parents about.

I ended up drinking four bottles of beer in total. I had planned to stop after one, but they kept coming and I kept accepting without thinking too much about it. It was when I noticed myself slurring my words that I realized I probably had enough.

Ricky and his cousins were still talking and laughing and having a great time. I felt the sudden urge to use the toilet. I stood up and had to hold my hands out in front of me to steady myself. Everything was swaying. Ricky noticed and quickly held out his hands to catch me.

"Are you okay?" he asked.

"Yea, I'm fine," I muttered. "Just need to go to the bathroom."

"Here," he said. "Let me help you."

"It's okay," I mumbled. "I can find it."

"You sure?" he asked, but I didn't reply, and I made my way out the door.

It was dark outside. There was a light coming from the party tent. I turned and walked in the opposite direction, up the hill to the house. A couple of times, I doubled over and almost walked on my hands and feet, but I caught myself and stood back up.

The door was open, despite nobody being around. I stumbled up the stairs, found our room, and made my way to the bathroom one door over. I was over the toilet for two seconds when it came out. Vomit. Thick and heavy.

I sat there for five minutes before I felt the courage to get up. I stripped off my clothes, tossed them to the side, and showered. The hot water helped, and the lightheadedness subsided slightly.

After that, I don't remember anything more. I woke up early. Ricky was beside me, in the same clothes he'd been wearing the night before. He must have been too drunk to bother changing.

His arm was over me and I pushed it off so that I could sit upright. I put my head in my hands. I felt ill. My head was throbbing, and I had a nasty taste in my mouth. I realized I forgot to brush my teeth the night before.

I got up and took another shower, brushing my teeth this time. I felt better as I stepped out of the shower. I looked in the mirror and noticed some hair growing on my upper lip. I raised my arm to examine my armpit hair. I would need to start shaving soon.

I threw on a pair of clean underwear and went back to bed. I laid there and waited until Mrs. Vergara came to our room and told us to get ready. Ricky got up and after he showered, we both got dressed. It was the morning of the wedding ceremony. I found a pair of black dress pants and a white dress shirt. Ricky wore something similar.

After a quick breakfast, we all loaded up into Uncle Josef's jeepney. There were about twelve of us. Mrs. Vergara and the other ladies were dressed in beautiful dresses, and they all wore beautiful jewelry and heavy makeup. The boys were in dress clothes, similar to what Ricky and I wore.

We drove fifteen minutes to what was the largest church I had seen in my life. It was massive.

The exterior was white marble with a blue hue that ran up the doorposts and lined the windows. It was like nothing like I had ever seen before.

There were a handful of churches in my hometown, including one Catholic church, but none looked anything like this.

The interior was even more remarkable than the exterior. I was struck by how bright it was. Gold adorned almost every object imaginable. I took in the beauty of the stained glass windows that lined both walls. At the front where the pulpit stood, there was a basin draped with a purple cloth. On the wall hung three crucifixes and a sculpture of the virgin Mary.

It was beautiful, but odd and mysterious at the same time. I followed Mrs. Vergara's direction and took a seat beside Ricky and his family on a pew. It was wood and hard. The pews at my home church had cushions.

Everything was different, but I took it in, and appreciating the beauty of it. As I looked around, another thought crossed my mind. In my church, we were always taught about the sin of money, or greed. We were taught that the church should be a witness to the local community, and to help those in need. There was much hypocrisy in my church, but that was one thing they were consistent about. Seeing all of this gold, and other signs of exuberant wealth, made me feel queasy to my stomach, but I was in awe at the same time.

I attended many weddings in my life, but they were nothing like this one. Besides the grandeur of it all, the ceremony itself took over an hour. About twice as long as weddings back home.

As I watched the bride come down the aisle, dressed in a beautiful white dress with a satin veil, I thought about whether I would ever get married. My parents always talked to me about getting married, and about the importance of remaining sexually pure until my wedding night. They talked about how God had the perfect woman planned for my future, and it was up to me to wait for her.

Sometimes I still grappled with the idea that I was gay. I looked over at Ricky sitting beside me. It was one thing to have this secret relationship with him, but it was quite another to think about getting married.

Is that something that I could do? Get married? Have a husband, just like this woman was about to have? I shuddered inside. That was something that I could never do. Getting married. Living openly as a gay man. Maybe having a couple of children. Somehow.

No. It was one thing to do this in secret. It was quite another to proclaim to the world, to everyone I knew, that I was gay. That was something that I couldn't do. Never. The way my parents talked about homosexuality, I was sure that they'd cut off all contact with me if they ever found out. I couldn't allow that to happen.

I pushed these thoughts out of my head and looked up at the groom, who was preparing to receive his wife. I didn't understand all the rituals that I witnessed. They lighted candles. There was a coin toss. There was something with coins, anyway. A priest conducted Mass. Finally, the bride and groom exited the church as they were officially introduced as husband and wife, and people threw grains of rice at them as they ran out. Not as colorful as confetti, but it was an interesting sight to see.

Back at the house, everyone was busy preparing for the wedding reception. It would be held across the street, in the same field as the party the night before. The tent was still up, and people were setting up chairs and tables, and they were putting out flower displays on each table. It looked similar to back home, but different at the same time.

Ricky and I helped ourselves to a generous helping of various Filipino dishes. I loved the food, and so I was in my element. Ricky's cousins joined us, and we ate together. I could tell that some kids looked hungover. I had a lingering headache as well. I knew then that I wouldn't drink again.

After we finished eating, Ricky indicated he wanted to go to the house, so I followed him back up the hill and to our room.

"What's up?" I asked as we both sat down on the bed. I looked at him with a smile, leaned in, and kissed him more passionately than I had ever done before.

I brought my hand around the back of his head and held him there. I ran my hand through his hair as we continued to make out. My thoughts went back to what I was thinking about earlier. Weddings. I wondered if maybe I could get married. I could see myself with someone like Ricky for the rest of my life. If I closed my eyes and thought hard enough, it seemed plausible.

When we finally broke apart, Ricky had a mischievous smile on his face.

"What?" I asked.

"Here," he said. He bent over and dug in his bag, pulling something out. When he showed me his hand, I saw it was the condom that Ronaldo gave me.

I took a deep breath as I looked at it. I took it and felt the plastic wrapping.

"Are you ready?" Ricky asked me.

I had to think for a moment. This was something I wanted. But there was something holding me back. Something that made me hesitate. I couldn't quite put my finger on it.

"Well?" Ricky said. He was staring at me with a questioning look.

"Okay," I said. "Let's do it."

I was fumbling with the buttons as I took my shirt off. Ricky didn't seem to be shaking at all. He had completely stripped by the time I was tossing my shirt to the side. He laughed.

"Here," he said, and he pulled my pants down. I pushed down my underwear and threw them to the side. Soon I was lying on top of him. I kissed him. I felt him. I ran my hands over his body, taking it all in with my fingertips.

I had a warm and fuzzy feeling inside. Even so, the uncomfortable beating of my heart seemed to get louder.

"You okay?" Ricky asked. I was anxious and it must have been obvious from the look on my face.

"I'm okay," I replied.

"Then what are we waiting for?" he asked. I wanted to wait another minute or two. I still wasn't sure if I was ready. I kissed him again, and he wrapped his arm around my neck.

It was so intense, and with my heart pounding in my ear, I didn't hear the door behind me open.

"What is this?" I heard someone say. The voice was stern. Ricky and I both desperately grabbed bedsheets to cover ourselves with.

Mrs. Vergara was standing in the doorway. I had never seen her look so furious before. "Get dressed and come downstairs, now!" she said, almost shouting. She turned around and marched out, slamming the door behind her.

At that moment, I wanted to die. My chest hurt. My throat hurt.

Then everything became numb. I tried to speak, but nothing came out. I looked at Ricky. Panic was written all over his face, too.

I stepped onto the floor and pulled my underwear back on. Ricky did the same. We tossed our dress clothes to the side and changed into casual clothes. Shorts and a T-shirt. I struggled to put how I felt into words, but the main emotion was fear. I was scared. More scared than I had ever been in my life.

Ricky looked even more scared than me. He was always the confident one. Always collected and cool. It wasn't encouraging to see the state he was in at that moment. I wanted to squeeze his hand. Give him a kiss. Comfort him in some small way. But I was too scared to touch him now.

I opened the door, and we both stepped out. My parents were going to hear about this. I knew it. What was going to happen when I got home? That worried me more than anything that the Vergaras could say or do.

Would they not let me back at their house again? Forbid Ricky and me from seeing each other? My head was so full of thoughts when we sat down at the table. Mrs. Vergara sat on the other side, across from us. Fortunately, there wasn't anyone else around. I was surprised. There were tears in her eyes. She stood up, walked over to me, and gave me a tight hug. I was confused. I wasn't sure what to think of this.

"We have a lot to talk about," she said. I nodded. Nodded and waited to see what she had to say.

ACKNOWLEDGEMENT

I want to give a big shout-out to my editor, Liz, who did a great job in helping me get my manuscript to where it is. This story was very personal, and I feel that she handled it with sensitivity and care.

And to my cover designer, Hedri, who again created an awesome work of art.

And last but not least, thank you very much to all of my readers and supporters. I appreciate you all. You're what keeps me writing.

Lots of love,
Steven Lundle

ABOUT THE AUTHOR

Steven Lundle

Steven is a filmmaker and author from the small hamlet of Rochfort Bridge, Alberta, Canada. He has been writing since childhood, and mainly writes horror and fantasy. Being a member of the LGBT community, but also having been raised in a conservative Christian, he likes to explore those themes as well. He currently lives in Phnom Penh, Cambodia with his dog, Romeo.

BOOKS IN THIS SERIES

ASHAMED

Ashamed

"I found myself always wanting to be with him, but was it more? Was I developing a crush on him? No, I couldn't be. If there was anything I knew, it was that homosexuality was one of the worst sins out there."

These were some of the questions plaguing 14-year-old Jeremiah, who lives in a small conservative town where he attends a strict fundamentalist Christian school. His parents hold onto the same values.
To add to the strain of things, he finds himself conflicted about his feelings for his classmate.
He knows better. Being gay is a sin. Can fundamentalist Christianity stand in the way of blooming romance?

Based on the author's own experiences, Ashamed is a fictitious story of a young boy trying to navigate the world of Christian Fundamentalism while struggling with his own sexuality.

BOOKS BY THIS AUTHOR

The Doll: And Other Short Stories

A collection of short dark stories about childhood fears, loneliness, and loss.
- Olivia receives a doll, but something seems off
-Rocky is having issues with a strange kid at daycare.
-Timmy sees things as he comes to terms with the death of his grandmother.
-Amiya desperately tries to find her friends who have disappeared in Tokyo.
-And what's behind that door that keeps reappearing in a dream?

"The Doll: and other short stories" is a collection of stories that deal with the dark and the supernatural.

The stories included in this anthology are:
The Doll
The Ward
The Game
The Door
The Street

Printed in Great Britain
by Amazon